THE SILK ROMANCE

The night Sophie Challoner spends together in Paris with handsome racing driver Jean-Luc Olivier seems to Sophie like a fairytale — but she knows she has no part in Jean-Luc's future. She made her dying mother a promise, so one night of happiness is all Sophie allows herself. However, Jean-Luc is determined to find out why she left him, and engineers a student placement Sophie can't refuse. Unwillingly, she finds herself back in France, thrown together once again with Jean-Luc . . .

HELENA FAIRFAX

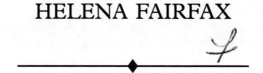

THE SILK ROMANCE

Complete and Unabridged

LINFORD
Leicester

First published in Great Britain in 2013

First Linford Edition
published 2015

C460566163

*A catalogue record for this book is available
from the British Library.*

ISBN 978–1–4448–2512–1

Published by
F. A. Thorpe (Publishing)
Anstey, Leicestershire

Set by Words & Graphics Ltd.
Anstey, Leicestershire
Printed and bound in Great Britain by
T. J. International Ltd., Padstow, Cornwall

This book is printed on acid-free paper

To Joe.
Wish you were here.

Acknowledgements

Thanks to my husband, Bob, for believing I could write a book and for being so excited about everything.

1

A deep voice reverberated around the empty chapel, bringing Sophie to a halt in the doorway. Outside, sunlight streamed over a group of black-clad mourners lingering in the memorial gardens. For a moment, she was tempted to let her feet carry her on, to pretend she'd heard nothing and escape into the Parisian sunshine . . . but that would be the act of a coward. She steeled herself, casting a last, longing glance at the departing mourners before making a slow turn to face the speaker.

'I am sorry for your loss, Mademoiselle Challoner.' The owner of the voice was standing in the aisle, in the semi-darkness of the deserted chapel of rest. The sunlight streaming in from the high windows fell in motes on his broad shoulders, leaving his features in shadow. When he stepped forward, a beam of dusty light lit up the brilliant blue eyes she remembered. He stretched out one strong hand. After a moment's hesitation, Sophie slipped her cold fingers into his.

'I assume I should still address you as mademoiselle?'

Sophie watched in silence as his blue eyes swept down to her ringless left hand.

'So you didn't marry, after all?' he persisted.

She felt the heat begin to mount in her cheeks and forced herself to speak. 'No, I . . . ' She pulled her hand out of his and began again. 'I didn't marry. Thank you for coming today. It was good of you to remember my grandmother.'

She made the mistake of lifting her eyes to his. He was regarding her with the same faintly contemptuous expression he had worn when her grandmother had first introduced them all those years ago. Sophie was grateful for the veil she wore. It masked the flush she could feel deepening. She turned to go.

'Mademoiselle Challoner.' His voice halted her again. He stepped past her, into the sunlight pouring through the door. And now Sophie was no longer able to prevent awareness flooding through her. Alone in the chapel, he had created an inescapable intimacy. His position blocked her exit, his stance confident and assured. Sophie remembered only too well how determined he could be. She looked up to find him gazing at her with a curiosity she found far more unnerving than his previous contempt. She flicked her gaze over his shoulder, her heart beginning to thump.

'Sophie,' he said softly.

Sophie closed her eyes. A formal *Mademoiselle Challoner* was almost bearable, but the intimate use of her first name brought a rush of memories that threatened to overpower her. With an effort of will she forced her eyes open, subduing the pounding in her throat.

'I don't think we have anything to say to one another.' Her words were too rapid, too high-pitched. He registered her reaction with a flick of his head but didn't move from the doorway. Sophie looked beyond him, searching for some means of escape, and noticed her brother at the tail-end of the crowd moving slowly out of the chapel gardens.

'Jack,' she called, her voice shrill with relief. She lifted one slim white hand to beckon him to her rescue. Beside her she heard a low, defeated laugh as the gentleman stepped back. She didn't look again in his direction.

Her brother, tall and gawky in his ill-fitting suit, turned and hurried toward them. Sophie performed the introductions, trying not to let the relief show in her voice.

'This is my brother Jack, monsieur. Jack, this is — '

'It's Jean-Luc Olivier. I recognised you straight away.' Jack thrust one long, slim hand from the worn cuffs of his jacket. 'But I didn't know you knew our grandmother.'

Jean-Luc accepted the recognition without comment. Of course, he was used to being recognised. He offered Jack his hand pleasantly.

'My uncle was an old friend of your grandmother's. I am sorry for your loss. Unfortunately, my uncle was too ill to attend, so I've come alone. I knew your grandmother myself.' He turned to Sophie, the charming smile vanishing. 'But perhaps we should say I am more a friend of her family.'

There was the lightest mocking inflection on the word *friend*. Sophie raised her chin at that, but Jean-Luc carried on, reaching inside the pocket of his dark suit.

'I am happy to see you again after all this time, mademoiselle. Here is my card. If you need anything — anything at all — get in touch.' He pressed the card into her hand. '*Au revoir*, mademoiselle. We'll meet again.'

He nodded, his final words an ambiguous mix of civility and threat, then strode away, the gravelled path crunching under his footsteps. Jack stared after him, jaw wide open.

'You know Jean-Luc Olivier?' he asked, astounded. 'And you never told me?'

Sophie shrugged, hugging her black jacket around her. She was watching the strong set of Jean-Luc's powerful shoulders as he walked away and wondering why, instead of feeling relief, every atom in her treacherous body was willing him to turn back.

'I met him years ago, at my eighteenth birthday party,' she said. 'You know, the one Grand-mère organised for me in Paris. The one you said you didn't want to go to because it would be full of snobs and rubbish celebrities, and you'd actually sooner stay at home and practise your violin.'

She raised her eyebrows in mock anger, but Jack ignored her. He was still staring wistfully after the retreating figure.

'But I had no idea he'd be there,' he protested. 'He's one of the most famous racing drivers in the world.'

'Well, you were invited.' She tapped his arm affectionately. 'Sometimes I think you love that violin more than me. Anyway,' she continued, her gaze drawn to the retreating figure, 'Jean-Luc doesn't race anymore. He's retired.'

'And how do you know that?' Jack's eyes widened.

Sophie turned helplessly as her brother's quick mind ticked over. Jean-Luc's handsome figure was disappearing down the drive. It was obvious Jack was putting two and two together.

'I don't believe it,' he said. 'You and Jean-Luc Olivier?'

Sophie gave a groan. Luckily, she was saved from further astute questioning by the approach of one of her grandmother's friends. She turned to accept more condolences, only to see with horror that Jean-Luc had still not left. He was deep in conversation with their father at the exit to the gardens.

She wondered what her guileless father was talking about and quivered. Her gentle father would be no match for a man like Jean-Luc, whose shrewd gaze just then met hers across the rest of the funeral stragglers. She looked away hastily. It wasn't until the last of the funeral guests said their goodbyes that Jean-Luc finally disappeared.

Their father was waiting patiently for them by the gate. Sophie turned to take her brother's arm and realised she was still clutching Jean-Luc's card in her hand. She lifted it up, registering for the first time that it was not the usual white or cream board, but solid gold. Her eyes flashed.

'Bling, bling,' she snorted. She tossed the card resolutely into the nearest litter bin, without reading the text, and walked on to join their father.

'Sophie, what do you think you're doing?' her brother hissed behind her. 'Why are you throwing that card away?'

She shrugged and turned away without speaking.

★　★　★

On the other side of the yew hedge surrounding the gardens, the object of Sophie's scorn sat behind the wheel of his car. He watched the family leave the chapel grounds, Sophie between her father and Jack, her hand tucked protectively in her father's arm. She had removed her close-fitting hat and veil and was carrying it in her left hand. Her thick, dark hair fell in abundance to her waist. Her face was pale and weary. As she grew nearer, she lifted her head and caught sight of him. For a split second, her incredible violet eyes rested on his face. Impossible to guess the emotion that lay behind that gaze. Fear? Longing? And then the trio moved on. In his rear-view mirror, Jean-Luc caught a glimpse of the determined set of Sophie's shoulders as she walked away from him down the tree-lined avenue. She didn't look back.

★　★　★

A few weeks after the funeral, back in London, Sophie got off the number 94 bus outside college and sighed with relief. The sun might shine brighter in her grandmother's native Paris, but Sophie was glad to be home, even if that meant putting up with overcast skies and drizzle. Sophie missed her grandmother dearly, but she didn't miss her grandmother's carelessly snobbish friends, the shallowness of her circle, their endless casual encounters . . . and she didn't miss men like Jean-Luc Olivier.

She gave an irritated shake of her head at the direction her thoughts were taking her. She had commitments now, and her grandmother's glamorous world had no part to play in keeping them. And she had been a fool to get involved with Jean-Luc Olivier in the first place. No matter how often that Frenchman appeared in Sophie's dreams, and no matter how often he smiled at her there, trying to make her feel she was part of his world, his life had nothing to do with hers or the reality of caring for her family. And just now she had her future employment to think of. If she didn't focus on her studies, her family would soon have no money coming in.

She put her bag over her head to keep off the rain and made a run for the college door. Her appointment with her tutor was at two, and it wouldn't do to be late.

Mr Barnes' normally stern features relaxed into a smile when she put her head round his door.

'So, back from Paris at last.' He got up to greet her. 'You've been having a hard time of it, eh?'

'Yes, I'm sorry I missed the start of term. I had to stay in Paris to see my grandmother's lawyers and sort out her affairs.'

Perhaps the strain of recent weeks showed in Sophie's pallor. Mr Barnes, not normally noted for his compassion for his students, appeared to sympathise. He knew Sophie had a lot on her shoulders.

'It's not going to be easy catching up with all the study you've missed. And your work placement will be quite a challenge. Think you'll be up to it?'

Sophie nodded. She'd put her heart and soul into getting onto her course. Now she was about to start work experience in France, and she was determined to make a success of it.

'Actually, I'm really looking forward to it.' She smiled, a genuine smile, for the first time in what seemed to her like months. 'And I hear I'll be going to Lyon. Is that right?'

Mr Barnes took his seat again. 'Well, you're right to be excited. You've certainly struck lucky with this one.'

He pulled a glossy brochure from his briefcase and pushed it across the table.

'But let me warn you, your place-ment is no soft option. The man you'll be working for has very high standards. Luckily, I could tell him quite sincerely that you were this year's top student.'

Sophie accepted the compliment

with a grin, and reached out eagerly across the table. Embossed in gold on the front cover of the brochure were the words *Pascha Silks*. The main shot showed a model striding down a catwalk, her stick-thin figure swathed in glorious red silk. Behind her was a blitz of flash photography and A-list celebrities. Sophie turned the cover curiously.

'This will be a fantastic experience for you. The company is a textbook example of how to turn round an ailing business,' Mr Barnes enthused. 'Pascha Silks produces some of the most fashionable textiles in the whole of Europe. The quality is high, and the MD's standards are also very high. We've been trying to get a student into this business for quite a while. Fortunately, this year there was no problem at all. The owner would consider only one student, and that student had to be you.'

Sophie sat stock still, her hand frozen in mid-air, her attention riveted to the brochure in front of her.

'Did you understand what I just said, Sophie?'

She gradually tore her gaze away from the open page and returned to her surroundings, eyes hazy.

'No, I don't.' Her gaze dropped back to the brochure she was holding rigidly in one hand. 'You mean he asked for me by name?'

On the inside cover of the brochure was the headshot of a strikingly good-looking man whose eyes pierced the camera with an intense blue. Underneath, in bold type, were the words *Monsieur Jean-Luc Olivier, Managing Director*.

Sophie looked up at her tutor again and spoke more forcefully. 'I'm sorry, actually I really don't understand.' Her voice rang loudly in her own ears. The photo in front of her was becoming a blur.

'Are you well, Sophie? Shall I fetch you a glass of water?'

Sophie barely noticed her tutor hurry away from his desk. She looked down again to find the azure eyes she had seen a few weeks previously gazing directly at her from the open page. She traced a hand over the picture. His hair was short. When they'd met four years ago, his hair had touched the collar of his leather jacket. Sophie had a sudden, vivid memory of reaching her hand up to grasp the back of his head. She cut off the thought and drew her hand back quickly from the picture as though it had burnt her.

The photographer had captured Jean-Luc with one of his rare smiles, his teeth white against his tan and faint laughter lines around his eyes. He looked extraordinarily handsome. Sophie put both her hands in her lap and clenched them. She must be more tired and strained than she thought. The blood was mounting to her cheeks in waves, leaving her feeling flushed and slightly feverish.

Her tutor reappeared from nowhere with a glass of water, and Sophie sipped at it gratefully.

'Are you sure you're up to this,

Sophie?' Mr Barnes was hovering behind his desk. 'I know you've had a lot on your plate recently, but it's not like you to succumb to nerves. I've always thought you a very resilient young woman.'

'I'm sorry,' she said, with a calmness she was far from feeling. 'I'm just a little overtired. Obviously I recognise Monsieur Olivier. I just hadn't realised . . . ' She picked up the brochure again, at a loss how to explain the scale of her astonishment. 'I hadn't realised this was his business,' she finished lamely.

'Well, why would you? He took over his family's silk mill four years ago, after he retired from Grand Prix racing.'

Of course she'd known he'd retired. The news had grabbed all the headlines. But she'd always imagined him retiring to the beaches in the south of France with his millions and a Ferrari. And a couple of designer blondes.

She pressed the icy water glass

16

against her cheek. None of it made any sense.

'Did you say he asked for me by name?' She wondered what Mr Barnes made of this strange request and tried to keep the question nonchalant.

Mr Barnes didn't seem to think it unreasonable that a business owner would want to take on a student as talented as Sophie. 'We sent him the CVs of our top students,' he said. 'At first he refused to take on anyone, as he has refused every year, but a few weeks ago he got on the phone personally. He wanted to take you, and only you. I explained that the placement would be delayed because of your grandmother's death, but he refused to take anyone else. Said he was prepared to wait as long as it took for you to finish sorting out your grandmother's affairs in Paris.'

Far from clearing matters up, her tutor's answer had only increased Sophie's bewilderment. The blue eyes in the photo were smiling back at her with an infuriating calm. She had the strong sensation of being manipulated. He had discovered where she was; and for reasons she couldn't begin to guess at, and in spite of the callous way she'd left him, he wanted to see her again after four years of silence.

'What if I don't take up the placement?'

Her tutor's brows drew together in a flash. 'Not take it? That would be insane. A moment ago you were excited about going to Lyon. Why on earth would you turn down a brilliant opportunity?'

He was right. What reason could she give? *Because I've slept with Jean-Luc Olivier, and I deliberately made him think I was a slapper?* She imagined herself saying the words out loud for one ridiculous moment and shook her head hopelessly. No one would even believe it. Jean-Luc Olivier was a champion racing driver who had a stream of glamorous girlfriends, including film stars and singers. He was a hero to millions of sports fans, and his face was recognised around the world. Sophie Challoner was a penniless student whose face was barely recognised in her own street. Who would ever believe they'd once spent the night together?

Her tutor broke in with unusual gentleness on her thoughts. 'Is it your father, is that it?' he asked. 'Is he still ill?'

'Oh no, no.' Sophie looked up then. 'He's been well for months now. It's taken a while, but he finally seems to be through the worst of his depression. I think he'll be okay with my brother whilst I'm away.'

'Well, what then?'

Sophie's expression fell.

'Let me tell you the position,' her tutor continued, pressing his fingertips together. 'If you don't complete a work-related project, it will be taken very seriously by the board of examiners. You will fail to graduate.'

Sophie swallowed. She had no idea why Jean-Luc Olivier wanted her to work for him. If he really wanted to see her again after that night — and from the look on his face when she'd walked out of their hotel room, she doubted that very much — why had he made no effort to contact her all the times she was in Paris? Why wait until now? It made no sense, but Sophie found that she had no interest in uncovering his motives. She was being manipulated and outmanoeuvred, and she didn't enjoy the feeling one bit. No one had told Sophie Challoner what to do since her mother died, leaving her in charge of her family. She lifted her head.

'I was last year's top student, you said it yourself. I know it's late in the term, but I can find a different placement. I'll just work twice as hard.'

Mr Barnes frowned. 'It's not as easy as that. If you work for this guy this year, there's every chance he will take another student from us next year and the year after. If you don't take up this offer, you'll ruin the chances for future students of working with Jean-Luc

Olivier. Student placements like this are damn hard to come by.'

Sophie realised the truth of this with a sinking heart. Jean-Luc's inscrutable face looked up, smiling, from the photo. She swallowed. After a moment, she raised her head and forced a smile.

'I suppose that means I don't have much choice, then, do I?' She picked the brochure up off the table. 'You'd better tell me all about it. I've missed a couple of weeks when I should have been researching this place, and I've a feeling I'm going to need to stay on my toes. I don't want to let Monsieur Jean-Luc Olivier catch me out.'

Not a second time, anyway, she promised herself.

* * *

Later that night, as she was sorting through her things for her return to France, her father poked his head round her bedroom door.

'All sorted then, Sophie?' His voice

was cheerful, but she knew the effort it was costing him to let her go. Although Jack would be there to look after him, he would miss her for the two months she was away. She reached up and kissed his cheek.

'Yes, it's all sorted,' she said softly. 'Come in, I'll tell you all about it whilst I'm packing.'

Her father sat down at the old school desk where Sophie had done her homework in happier times, in the days when her mother had been alive and before her father began his slow slide into illness. It seemed like a lifetime ago. She pressed the Pascha Silks brochure into his hands.

'Looks good, doesn't it?' she said brightly.

Her father turned the cover. The owner's imposing presence was even more arresting in the smallness of Sophie's bedroom.

'Jean-Luc Olivier,' he said. 'That's a surprise. You've done well there, Sophie. His company's silks are doing really well.

Seems they were on all the catwalks at London Fashion Week.'

Sophie looked down at her father's greying head affectionately.

'Dad, you always amaze me.' She laughed. 'I didn't know you read the fashion pages.'

Her father grinned back. 'Well, it's more the sporting pages I'm interested in. He was brilliant on the racing track until he retired. It's a strange coincidence, though, isn't it?'

'Coincidence?' Sophie echoed uncomfortably. She turned her back and carried on packing.

'Yes. He was at your grandmother's funeral. Didn't you see him? His uncle was a friend of your grandmother's.'

Sophie made a business of folding and re-folding one of her pencil skirts.

'Actually, I had already met him before the funeral,' she said eventually, hoping her voice sounded casual. Her night with Jean-Luc Olivier definitely belonged in the category of Things Not To Discuss With Your Father.

'Really? When?'

'You know the eighteenth birthday party Grand-mère wanted to throw for me in Paris? He was there.' Sophie finally placed the skirt neatly in her case, and began folding a shirt without turning round.

'Oh, of course. That time when your grandmother thought she'd introduce you to all the rich husband material in France.' He suddenly laughed out loud. 'Perhaps she thought Jean-Luc Olivier might propose.'

Sophie laughed too; a small, empty sound. 'Even Grand-mère couldn't think that. Jean-Luc Olivier has a different girl on his arm every week.'

'Anyway,' her father continued, 'your grandmother's isn't the place to find a husband. Remember that family friend of hers who visited once?'

'Do you mean Louis?' Sophie asked. 'That was years ago, Dad. It was a teenage crush.'

'And he dumped you as soon as he saw where you lived. Jumped-up snob.

How dare he think you weren't good enough?'

Sophie's expression lost its sparkle. Although she could joke with her father, the experience was still painful. In her schoolgirl innocence, she had imagined her first boyfriend's love for her would transcend the fact that, unlike their wealthy grandmother, the Challoner branch of the family lived on a housing estate in north London. The reality was that as soon as the bourgeois Louis Saint-Jacques had seen their litter-filled street, with its boarded-up shop on the corner, he had rushed back to Paris with a curt goodbye, leaving lasting damage to Sophie's psyche. Not only that, to excuse the callous way he'd behaved, he had spread vicious lies amongst her grandmother's friends, saying he'd had to leave London because Sophie was only after his money.

Sophie looked out of the window of her room, where the remains of the daylight were falling onto the shabby

25

gardens. Below her, her old neighbour, Mr Khan, was clearing up the broken glass left by youths the night before. She liked Mr Khan. She liked a lot of her neighbours, but Foxglove Avenue was a long way from the yachts and villas and ski resorts in which her grandmother's friends were found.

'Yeah, well . . . ' She shrugged her shoulders, carefully nonchalant. 'I've learnt my lesson since bringing Louis here. Don't mix with Grand-mère's friends.'

Her father harrumphed in agreement.

'Jean-Luc seems a decent enough chap, though,' he continued blithely. 'And was really very pleasant at the funeral. We spoke a lot about you, actually.'

'Really?' Sophie's eyes widened at this and she turned round, all pretence at casualness forgotten. 'What did he say?'

'Oh, nothing much. He thought you'd got married, for some reason.'

Sophie winced again at the childish lie she'd told him all those years ago. Jean-Luc hadn't made it easy for her to leave that hotel room, and a make-believe fiancé had been the only excuse she could think of. She still remembered the look of disgust on his face as she closed the door.

Her father continued, 'I put him straight about that. Not that he's husband material himself.' He let out a loud guffaw.

The penny finally dropped for Sophie. She put her hands on her hips.

'Dad, what else did you talk about? Did you tell him the name of my college?'

A look of confusion crossed her father's face. Sophie sighed. It was no use blaming her dad. He would have been no match for Jean-Luc. Sophie herself had been no match for him. Her father had handed over the means to engineer her placement, in all inno-cence, and Jean-Luc had made full use of the information.

So, that explained how it had happened. But it still didn't explain why.

The sound of the front door slamming, followed by a tuneful whistling in the hallway, interrupted her dark train of thought.

'Jack's back from college,' she said unnecessarily. Her brother was a welcome excuse to cut short the conversation; but before she could leave the room, her father held out a tentative hand to halt her.

'I'm sorry for all the trouble I've given you, love.'

'Dad!' she protested. 'It wasn't your fault. You couldn't help being ill. It's just one of those things.'

'I could have been stronger,' he said. 'When your mother died, I — '

'Ssh, Dad, I know.' There was nothing either of them could say about her mother's slow death from cancer. Nothing that could take away the constant grief. Her father released her and picked up her mother's photo from the desk where Sophie kept it. It had been taken in Paris, when her mother still lived there before their marriage took her to England. A vibrant woman, she smiled radiantly from the frame, long black hair tied back in a scarf, the world with all its possibilities still in front of her.

'You look so much alike. You have her beautiful eyes,' her father said softly. 'Your mother asked you to look after Jack and me, and you've worked so hard for both of us. She would have been proud of you.'

Sophie's eyes welled up. 'Oh, Dad. She'd be proud of all of us.'

'We'll be okay, love. You go and show Jean-Luc Olivier what you're made of.'

2

Sophie stood on the street opposite the Pascha Silks mill in Lyon's historic La Croix-Rousse district, her heart bumping, holding on to the memory of her family's loving farewell a little desperately. During the past few days, she had read the company brochure from cover to cover and done as much groundwork as she could, not confining her research just to the silk-weaving industry. She learned that Jean-Luc Olivier had had a privileged upbringing and been expensively educated at one of France's top private schools. He had retired from racing suddenly, at the height of his career. He was not married. It was impossible to discover if he was in a relationship. Recent photos showed him escorting various implausibly thin and beautiful women. There were no direct interviews and absolutely no clues to the man himself.

The building in front of her was just as impenetrable. Large gold letters spelled out the words *Pascha Silks* above the doorway, matching the stylish brochure. Sophie gazed up at the building's façade. Impossible to see what was happening behind all those windows. She shifted her shoulder bag, lifted her chin with bravery she was far from feeling, and began to cross the road.

★ ★ ★

Two storeys up, from his desk on the second floor, Jean-Luc broke off his telephone conversation and placed his mobile on the table. He moved nearer the window, narrowing his eyes against the light.

She was standing hesitantly on the other side of the road, a copy of the company brochure clutched to her chest. She was very primly dressed in a blouse and tight pencil skirt, her

31

luxurious black hair drawn back into a neat bun. She was still beautiful.

A slow smile tugged at the corners of his mouth. She had come, and his instincts had been right. She was nothing if not courageous. He followed her as she squared her shoulders and tilted her head determinedly. Looking right and left, she crossed the road towards the main entrance of the building and disappeared beneath him.

Jean-Luc turned to his desk, his smile replaced by a look of uncharacteristic self-doubt. They had both changed. The young English girl he had known four years ago had matured. He thought of the figure he had glimpsed through the window. She was more curvaceous, more womanly than the teenager he had known. He made the mistake of letting his thoughts dwell on that figure, and suddenly he was filled with the same adrenaline rush he had at the starting-line of every race. And the same determination to win, at all costs.

The phone on his oak desk purred softly.

'Mademoiselle Challoner, monsieur.' His receptionist hesitated over the English name.

'*Bon*, Annette. Send her upstairs to me.'

★ ★ ★

Downstairs in reception, Sophie clutched the brochure more tightly. The receptionist had offered her a seat, but she preferred to calm her nerves by inspecting the silks on show in the reception area. It was an exotic display. Brightly-coloured fabrics fell in dramatic folds from several stands arranged along one wall. Sophie reached out a hand to feel the softness of a peacock silk glide through her fingers. She was filled with an incredible sense of the surreal.

'Monsieur Olivier will see you now,' said the receptionist. 'Good luck.'

Sophie gave a small, tight nod in return, unable to smile. *That's me*

— *lucky*, she thought with dull irony when she reached the MD's door. A brass plaque stared at her coldly. JEAN-LUC OLIVIER. DIRECTEUR GÉNÉRAL.

She straightened her shoulders and knocked.

'Come in.' The deep, familiar voice came unhurried through the heavy door. Sophie hesitated just a fraction, before turning the brass handle and pushing the door wide.

He was silhouetted by the window, hands in his pockets, leaning back against the frame. Sophie registered again the change in his appearance. She was still expecting to confront his younger self, to see him in a leather jacket, his hair tousled, a silk shirt open at the neck. Instead, a sober suit and tie completed the sensation of the surreal. His face, the same she had known, yet curiously different, was dark and unsmiling against the white of his collar.

Sophie took in at a glance the office

desk, the neat rows of files, the computer humming softly in the corner. In spite of the trappings of convention, something in Jean-Luc's pose reminded her forcefully of the driven young man she had known. Neither of them moved. The powerful neck and shoulders were outlined against the light. It was a figure ready for action. A chill settled into Sophie's very bones. Perhaps realising she was poised for flight, Jean-Luc shifted suddenly and moved away from the window.

He held out his hand. 'Mademoiselle Challoner.' A slow, disarming smile spread, lighting his gaze with unexpected warmth. Sophie put her hand in his.

As soon as she felt the strength in his brown hand, she was thrown instantly to the night she had lain beside him, his powerful arms wrapped around her, pressed to the heat of him. Despite herself, she closed her eyes momentarily.

'Or perhaps I should call you Sophie?' he continued, looking down. 'Since we know each other so well.'

Sophie's eyes flew open. Now she knew for certain it had been a mistake to come. She tugged her hand out of his grasp. He let go of her immediately and stepped back, the harsh lines on his face softening.

'I'm sorry,' he said. 'That was unforgivable of me.'

Sophie stared at him blankly.

'Yes, I'm apologising. Is that so hard to believe?' The laugh that accompanied his question had a harsh edge. 'It was ungentlemanly of me. Let's start again. Please, sit down.'

Without waiting for her reply, he turned to sit behind his large oak desk, swivelling his leather chair to face her. When she did not move, he indicated the seat in front of him. For a few moments they regarded each other without speaking: Sophie's eyes still guarded, his own coolly determined. Eventually Sophie sat, warily, in the seat opposite his.

He smiled. The smile had an air of satisfaction that caused Sophie's hackles to rise.

'Why am I here?' she asked abruptly.

'I don't understand your question, mademoiselle.' He raised his dark eyebrows.

'I think you do understand. And I don't like being manipulated. Why here? Why now?'

Jean-Luc leaned forward, his expression faintly derisory. 'Were you expecting our encounter all those years ago to be free from repercussions? No one escapes the consequences of their actions, Mademoiselle Challoner.'

Sophie gasped, eyes widening in outrage. 'They were your actions as well as mine,' she said hotly. She knew straight away her words were a mistake. What she saw in his eyes caused her to flush bright red, the hot colour eradicating her pallor.

'Oh, I remember my actions very well.' His eyes were lit with a dangerous glow. 'As well as I remember yours.'

Sophie drew back. The memory of that night burned in her mind. Unlike Jean-Luc, she was struggling to keep her feelings under control. The heat in her cheeks refused to subside. She drew a deep breath.

'It was a long time ago. Why bring it back now?'

'When you get to know me better, you will realise I don't like mysteries. Now you, Mademoiselle Challoner, have turned out to be something of a mystery.'

'That's not true. There's nothing remotely mysterious about me.'

'Oh, but I think there is. A woman who passes herself off as a groupie, spends a passionate night with a stranger, then returns to London, telling him she is already engaged. The fiancé turns out to be a lie. Four years later the same woman reinvents herself as a model student and picture of respectability.'

'It's not invention. This is my life!'

'So I understand. But something doesn't quite ring true.' His eyes narrowed. 'What did you hope to gain from that night, mademoiselle? Your grandmother's friends called you a gold-digger. They say your family is in debt. Did you try and sell your story, was that it? A few thousand euros for a kiss-and-tell?'

'That's incredibly offensive.'

Jean-Luc merely shrugged. 'It's been tried by women in worse financial straits than you are.'

'I'm not in financial straits.' Jean-Luc's blue eyes were a lot more penetrating than Sophie remembered. Suddenly, it was desperately important that she show him no weakness, no dire need for money. She immediately compounded her lie with a greater one. 'My grandmother made me her heiress.'

As soon as the words had left her lips, she wondered what on earth had possessed her to say them. Her grandmother had left her with nothing at all. In fact, her grandmother had frittered away all her money in her final years trying to keep up the appearance of wealth. Sophie felt sorry for her grandmother. Insecurity had made her foolish and vain. Jean-Luc Olivier had no excuse for his arrogance. So, even knowing it was wrong, she sealed her lips on her lie and lifted her chin.

Jean-Luc refused to let the subject drop.

'Your tutor tells me your father has been ill. Is that right?'

Sophie folded her arms across her body in an unconsciously defensive gesture.

'What do you know about my family?' she asked, her words a sharp, protective staccato.

'I know your mother died when you were a teenager, and your father has been ill.' His voice was deadly quiet. 'I know it is you who pays for your brother's music lessons. I know you have no one left to protect you.'

His knowledge of her history shook Sophie to the core. For a moment she stared at him, rigid with shock. Then her nerves, strung to the limit since her grandmother's death, snapped into volatile little pieces. A match was lit to the loneliness within her and she leapt to her feet, violet eyes ablaze.

'How dare you threaten me! How dare you! I've lost my family and you dare to make threats. My family is nothing to you.' Her fear at her current helpless situation poured out of her in a torrent of useless, shaking rage. She knew she was out of control — the hot, angry tears welled and fell, blurring her vision, but she was powerless to stop.

'What do you want from me? Four years is a long time. I was young and reckless then, but not anymore!' She leaned over the desk in savage fury. 'I left you that night because I didn't want anything else to do with you, do you hear me? Nothing to do with you! And now leave my family alone,' she finished on a childish, shaking sob.

Her tormentor spun out of his chair and towered over her, his hands gripping her arms above the elbows, his eyes boring their piercing blue into hers.

'I'm not threatening you. *Calme-toi, chérie,*' he said urgently. Sophie drew in her breath in a shuddering gulp as she took in his meaning. He had called her his darling. The mask of formality had dropped, and he was holding her again. His mouth was so close to hers, she could almost touch it with her own. Her fury fell away as quickly as it had come, to be replaced by shaking gasps.

His own breathing equally uneven, Jean-Luc stared, horrified, at the tears rolling down her cheeks. She stiffened under the strength of his fingers. With a quiet expletive, he suddenly relaxed his hold on her.

For several seconds they stood in silence, Sophie straightening herself as Jean-Luc dropped his hands to his sides. The tears continued to flood her cheeks, and she reached a shaking hand to brush them away.

'*Tiens*, Sophie,' he said eventually,

putting his hand in his breast pocket and pulling out a neatly pressed handkerchief. 'Take this.'

She looked suspiciously at his outstretched hand, then snatched the snowy handkerchief and sat down, squeezing the white cloth to her eyes and saying nothing.

'I'm sorry,' Jean-Luc said gruffly after a time, and followed his apology with a humourless laugh. 'That's the second apology you've had from me in less than ten minutes. This is suspiciously like a habit.'

Sophie dropped the handkerchief from her face and took another shuddering attempt at controlling her breathing. She wondered what the staff and students at her college would think of her now — the unflappable Sophie Challoner, dissolved in tears on her first day at work. She was shaken by the realisation that there was something about Jean-Luc that reached right to the heart of her, stripping away her cool exterior. If this was the effect he had on her first afternoon, she dreaded to think what the next two months would bring.

She finally controlled herself enough to speak. 'I'm sorry, too. The past few weeks have been a strain.'

Jean-Luc digested her words, looking thoughtfully at the crumpled figure in front of him.

'*Écoute*, Sophie,' he said. 'I'm not threatening you. Or your family. On the contrary, I know things have been hard for you. I'm glad your grandmother left you provided for, but don't you think it would be better if you were not alone?'

'I'm not alone. I have my father and brother.'

'That's good to hear.' He continued to look at her steadily, but his tone lacked conviction, and his eyes were as shrewd as ever. Sophie twisted the handkerchief in her lap. Her grandmother had not left her provided for. She had nothing. Her father was too infirm himself to support her, and her brother was too young and too involved in his music studies to spare much time for anything else. For the moment, Sophie was alone, and there was no answer she could give that would convince Jean-Luc otherwise.

He sat back in his chair and smiled at her encouragingly. 'Your father and brother will have to do without you for a while. You're here with me, now.'

Sophie nodded. She knew very well that Jean-Luc had her where he wanted her. Men like Jean-Luc generally got what they wanted.

'You must forgive my suspicions, mademoiselle. My dealings with women have left me a little disillusioned. But I'm sure you're no opportunist.' He smiled, but in spite of the appearance of sympathy, his smile continued to hold a hint of chill. Sophie stiffened her shoulders, eyeing him warily.

'But we've talked enough. For now,' he continued. 'Let's get down to business.'

He picked up the sheet of foolscap which had been lying on the desk in front of him and carried on, single-mindedly banishing their previous conversation. 'This is an excellent, if unusual, CV, mademoiselle. The other students had nothing like your experience.'

'Really?' Sophie lifted her head, tears momentarily forgotten.

'You were successful at school, but you left at sixteen to become a secretary. Why was that?'

'It was good to be earning some money,' Sophie said, without elaborating. Jean-Luc's sharp gaze met hers again, but he appeared to accept her answer at face value.

'Eventually you were earning very good money.' He looked at the salary on her CV and raised his eyebrows. 'Very good money indeed, for one so young.'

'I started off in a small business. My boss and I got on really well. After a while, I got promoted.'

His eyebrows flew even higher. Once again, Sophie felt the full force of his perceptive gaze. 'I see,' he said. 'Getting on with the boss is often a step up the ladder.'

His insinuation brought Sophie's chin up instantly.

'My boss, Mrs Lawson,' she said, emphasising her boss's female status with satisfaction, 'thought I was highly competent. She was an excellent mentor. In fact, it was her idea for me to go back to college. She offered me promotion with her when I finish this placement.'

Her spirited response finally won a genuine smile and a small nod from him. 'And your tutor speaks very highly of you. If I didn't think you could do an excellent job here, I wouldn't have offered you a placement.'

Without waiting for her to answer, he bent to pick up a bundle of fabric swatches from beside his desk. Within moments, he was absorbed in a description of her role and his need for someone who could speak English to help win a contract in the US. The silks slid through his masculine hands as he spoke, the fabrics falling over his fingers in vibrant colours.

'There is a real role here for you and plenty to be done. When I took over from my uncle, the company was ailing. Now we are selling worldwide.' Sophie noted the unmistakeable pride in his voice. 'I promise you, your two months with me will be very rewarding.'

Two months with Jean-Luc. *Rewarding* was not the adjective Sophie would have used. It was a daunting prospect. It had taken all her resolve just to step through the door. She lifted her gaze from the fabric swatches he had passed to her, and registered again the changes in his physical appearance. She had already marked the faint lines beneath his eyes. The young, impetuous man she had known seemed on the surface to be gone. There was about him now a new steadiness, a strength that was indefinable.

Jean-Luc appeared to catch the way she was studying him and smiled. The smile lit up his face and brought back a trace of the young man she remembered, causing her treacherous heart to skip a beat.

'I've asked all the questions,' he said. 'What about you? Isn't there anything you'd like to ask?'

She hesitated. There was a lot she would like to know. Where to start? Her attention was drawn to a photo hanging on the wall behind Jean-Luc's desk. There in the gold frame was a picture of the Jean-Luc she'd known — a young racing driver, in team colours, high on the winner's podium. Dominating the photo was a trophy, held triumphantly aloft in one strong hand; in the other hand, a bottle of champagne overflowed in a froth of bubbles. A radiant smile split his tanned face, his brilliant eyes bursting with youthful enthusiasm. Sophie's gaze travelled slowly from the old photo back to Jean-Luc, a silent question hovering on her lips.

He raised an eyebrow. 'You want to

know how I got here. What became of the young man in the photo.'

Again, Sophie was caught by his perspicacity. She nodded. 'You had such a different career then, a different life. I'd like to know what's changed. Why are you here?'

She saw him frown and lifted her chin a little, the tears still faintly staining her cheeks. 'Or is that not the sort of question you meant?'

He met her gaze, accepting the faint hint of challenge before giving a small, unsmiling nod.

'It's only fair. You've every right to ask.' He leaned away from her, his seat tipping back slightly. For a long moment, he said nothing. His eyes were on some point above her head, his lips still. All mobility and expressiveness had left him. In the quiet office, an ineffable sadness descended. Sophie gazed wide-eyed at the sudden change in him. The youthful photo behind him smiled uncaring over his shoulder. His present-day features were etched in grief. She wondered what could possibly have happened in his past to cause such bleakness, and was filled with guilt for the challenging way she questioned him.

'Sometimes there are events that happen in life which are outside our control,' he said eventually.

Sophie noticed his fingers were clenched on the arms of his chair. Control would be important to a man of Jean-Luc's character. She couldn't imagine a situation outside his command, and wondered what terrible event had left him with such a feeling of impotence.

'But you asked me how I've changed,' he said finally. 'Perhaps I don't even know the answer myself. I'm not much given to introspection.' He pushed his chair back from the table. 'You might remember, I prefer action to words.'

His statement dispelled his sorrow, bringing a night full of memories vividly alive, so that in spite of the distance he had just made between them, they were both instantly flooded with physical awareness. Sophie felt her blood leap and saw an answering flash in those bright blue eyes. Of course she remembered. She remembered everything. It was the single most passionate experience of her life. Nothing and no one had ever come close.

'Sophie,' he said quietly.

She lifted her chin shakily, pushing away the lock which had fallen over her eyes. Moving with quick and cat-like grace, Jean-Luc left his chair to stand in front of her, placing himself between her and the door.

'Four years is a long time. We were both younger then.'

Sophie eyed him, full of mistrust. What did he mean by his words? That he had changed? In one respect, he was definitely the same man. He still had the extraordinary ability to organise events as he wanted them, despite all opposition. And she realised with dismay that she knew absolutely nothing about what had happened to Jean-Luc in those past four years. He had succeeded in keeping his private life just that. Intensely private. He positioned himself on the desk in front of her, his masculine thighs perilously close to her line of vision.

'*Écoute, chérie.* Four years ago I was that young man in the photo. I was young. I had money. I was hell-bent on having a good time, on and off the race track. That young man was my life, but now he's gone.'

'Do you mean you've changed?'

'Such deep questions.' He smiled, assessing her gravely. 'No, I haven't changed. Outwardly, the trappings have changed. But Jean-Luc Olivier, the man, not the famous driver, is still the same man he ever was.'

'In that case, I have another question for you.' Sophie lifted her head and looked at him with piercing directness. 'Why did you ask for me?'

Jean-Luc didn't pretend not to

understand. He returned her wide-eyed gaze with equal candour. 'I told you, I don't like mysteries. That morning you ran away from me.' He lowered his voice and drew his face nearer to hers, his smile taking the threat out of his mocking words. 'And no one runs away from me. Ever.'

Their eyes held a moment. Sophie registered the determination in his expression and, to her chagrin, was the first to look away, dropping her gaze to the crumpled handkerchief on her lap. She had no idea how to respond. She was outmanoeuvred and out of her depth, and Jean-Luc was fast depleting whatever inner reserves of strength she had. From somewhere, she managed to summon up enough will to reply tartly: 'Yes, I know. I remember the women crawling all over you at my eighteenth party. Doesn't it get a bit boring?'

'Depends on the woman,' Jean-Luc deadpanned. Sophie looked at him suspiciously. When she saw amusement flicker in his eyes, her lips lifted in a smile despite herself.

'Almost a smile,' he said with satisfaction. 'We've made progress. Now,' he stood up, towering over her, 'we can start with a clean slate. Shall I show you your office?'

He held her chair for her as she stood, their hands brushing together briefly. The tremor that passed between them was all the proof Sophie needed that the past could never be wiped clean, in spite of his assurance. The history was there between them. All she had to do was get through these next two months. And get through them without doing something else stupid she would regret.

Whatever she was feeling, Jean-Luc picked up on it with his usual astuteness. He kept an exaggerated distance as he led her into her office. A small, tidy room, filled with morning light, faced onto the street, its wooden shutters pushed open to the summer air.

'You see there is already a lot for you

to do.' He gestured toward the neat stack of papers piled up on the desk. The distance between them was now a good three feet. 'There are some documents here I'd like translated. And these will be useful background for you.' He reached above the computer and brought a bulging file down from the shelf in one strong hand. 'In here are samples of our marketing materials. If you could make a start targeting the US — I have a list of contacts — that would be a good beginning . . . ' He caught sight of her expression and stopped short.

'Well?' He raised his eyebrows impatiently. 'What is it?'

Sophie was getting her first taste of Jean-Luc Olivier's famous drive in action.

'The United States is a large country,' she said dryly. 'Do you think two months will be long enough?'

His lips twitched. 'Are you afraid of hard work?'

Sophie thought of the promise that

bound her to her mother. She thought of the many months she had spent working days as a secretary and evenings as a waitress, to help pay her father's debts after his business collapsed, and to keep her brother's music lessons going. Jean-Luc didn't know the half of it.

She shook her head. 'I don't mind hard work.'

'*Bon.*' Jean-Luc smiled. To his delight, a genuine smile appeared for a couple of seconds, transforming Sophie's tearstained features. Her red mouth widened and two enticing dimples appeared. He felt his heart leap. She had not smiled at him properly since she arrived in his office and it pained him to know he was the cause of such distrust. He was overwhelmed with the urge to reach for her. But maybe the flame in his eyes had flared too strongly, because instantly she took a step back. Her smile vanished, and she was gazing at him warily. He choked down his disappointment. Of course it was too soon — far too soon — to coax Sophie out of her mistrust. He had two months. Two months in which to understand the real reason she had left him, and to win her trust. As much as it went against the grain, he knew he would have to slow down and allow Sophie to approach him at her own pace. With an effort, he increased the distance she had made between them and turned toward the door.

'Good,' he said again gravely. 'Let's carry on with our tour.'

He held the door wide and waited for her to pass, noting she kept a careful distance, making sure not to touch. But maybe his cautious approach was beginning to pay off. Although Sophie was no longer smiling, the tension had gone from her shoulders and the faint strain from her face.

And, he noted dryly, at least she had still not run away.

3

The room they entered next was a complete contrast to Sophie's neat office. A vast mess of light and colours assaulted her as soon as Jean-Luc opened the door. The streaming sun lit up a jumble of coloured silks, open magazines and fashion books, torn sketches and designs, all littering the floor at random. A radio played pop music in one corner and overall lingered the delicious smell of croissants and strong coffee.

'How's it going, girls?' Jean-Luc called.

A young woman with dark hair turned from her computer, gold bands on her arm jangling gracefully as she moved. The screen she was working on showed a bright textile design of intricate yellow and green leaves.

'*Bonjour*, Monsieur Olivier.' Two

chocolate-brown eyes looked up at him, full of mischief.

'Sophie, this is Louisa. Louisa is one of our textile designers. Louisa, this is Sophie, our English student.'

''Allo, 'ow are you?' Louisa held out her hand, rolling the English consonants with a charming accent. Sophie took her hand in hers and smiled, instantly drawn.

'And this is Céline.' Jean-Luc indicated the far corner of the room, where a young girl with a shock of red hair was crouching, crossly examining a roll of silk. On seeing Jean-Luc, she lifted her head dramatically, hands held wide.

'Just look at this sample, monsieur. This is not at all how I wanted it made up. The colours are all wrong, and they've ruined my design.'

The young girl squeezed her eyes shut on an angry sob. A small, perfectly-formed tear forced its way out from between her long, black lashes to hover tragically on her high cheekbone.

An astonished Sophie watched Jean-Luc step carefully through the discarded sketches on the floor, handkerchief at the ready, to crouch down patiently by the girl's side. There couldn't have been a greater contrast between his strong, masculine body and the feminine backdrop the girls had made of their office. Other men would have felt intimidated, but Jean-Luc looked as composed and collected as he had in the masculine world of the pit stop.

'Now then, Céline, let's see what we can salvage,' he said calmly. 'Louisa, come here, what do you think?'

The next minute, the three heads were together, carefully inspecting the sample of silk. Céline's ready tears dried as they became engrossed in a technical debate on dyeing the yarn. The two girls jabbered excitedly.

Sophie, unable to join in the conversation, took advantage of their distraction to watch Jean-Luc in growing wonder. She would never have expected him to be capable of such patient restraint. Crouching his powerful figure beside the girls, he nodded from time to time as they gesticulated and argued with each other. Occasionally he would interrupt, bringing them gently but firmly back to the matter in hand. His lean brown fingers held the cloth lightly, the delicacy of the fabric highlighting the strength in his hands. Whilst the two girls swooped and picked up various cones of yarn like two little sparrows, he listened carefully, his large body still. After a while, he stood up, his wide shoulders against the light from the window.

'*Bon*,' he said decisively. 'So we have a plan. Don't take these things to heart, Céline.' He patted her reassuringly on the shoulder. 'Sometimes things go wrong, but it's important to find a solution.'

'Thanks for your help, monsieur.' Céline looked up at him with patent hero-worship.

The two girls chorused their good-byes as Jean-Luc left the room. Sophie turned to give them a friendly wave and was startled to see dark-haired Louisa checking out Jean-Luc's rear view. She caught Sophie's eye, winked and raised her fingers to her lips, as though about to wolf-whistle. Sophie broke into a smile and Louisa grinned back.

'Nice to have you with us,' she called.

Sophie left the room no longer feeling so alone. And she'd discovered that in his dealings with his staff, there was a considerate side to Jean-Luc, something she hadn't expected. But there was no time to reflect on this insight into his character, because he was already hurrying her down the corridor.

'Now, we just have time to pay a visit to our weavers,' he said. 'You must see how our silks are made.'

He strode ahead. When he reached the staircase, he began leaping down two at a time, his large body surprisingly light and agile, leaving Sophie to break into a run in order to catch up with him. Her slim heels and pencil skirt impeded her progress. Halfway down the stairs he came to a halt, leaning against the banister to wait for her. Slowly, she descended until she stood a couple of steps above him, the old wariness returning. He dropped his gaze to her feet, and then his eyes travelled with painful slowness from her violet-painted toes and long, bare legs, taking in her slim skirt and neat blouse, to rest finally on her face and search her expression. His features softened and there was a half-smile on his lips. Sophie gripped the banister, waiting.

'I remember the first time I saw you,' he said. Then, when she still did not speak, he added softly, 'You were standing at the top of a staircase that night, too. With just the same expression.'

Instantly, his words and his intensity transported Sophie back to the start of that unforgettable evening. Standing at the top of the staircase at the hotel in Paris, her grandmother by her side, welcoming her guests on her coming-of-age. The memory of a dark-haired Jean-Luc mounting the stairs toward her, his brilliant eyes fixed intently on hers. And she had thought he had forgotten. That it wouldn't have been important to him.

'Do you remember everything?' she asked huskily. Jean-Luc's eyes darkened, and she found herself leaning towards him, lips parted expectantly. Alone together, their bodies almost touching, the temptation to repeat that night, to forget the chasm that existed between their worlds, was overwhelmingly strong.

A heavy door slammed, and the sudden sound jolted Sophie back to reality. The memory of the promise she had made her mother slipped over her again, a well-worn mantle. She remembered Jean-Luc's iron determination, how easily he could sweep her away from her purpose, and she forced her expression to harden. He was staring at her, still with that same intensity. A wolf in sheep's clothing.

'I have grown up since we last met,' she said, injecting a coldness into her voice she did not feel.

Jean-Luc looked up into her closed expression and smiled patiently. She gripped the iron banister. She remembered all too well that underneath Jean-Luc's charm ran a core of steel. Even his eyes were a hard, metallic blue in the half-light of the stairwell.

He shrugged, seemingly making light of their conversation, and turned to go. At the bottom of the staircase, he looked back at her, still standing there.

'Grown up, do you say? On the contrary, mademoiselle, you are still very young. Your Miss Moneypenny outfit does not make you a grown up, chérie.'

Sophie's jaw dropped open.

'What did you say? Miss Moneypenny?' She smoothed her hands down her pencil skirt and walked quickly down the stairs toward him. It gave her a moment's gratification to see him look anxious, as though worried he had offended her. 'I'll have you know I'm creating a professional image,' she said primly.

'And I'm sure you'll do a professional job, Sophie.' He hesitated and then opened his mouth as though to add something further. Sophie looked at him expectantly, but whatever he had been about to say, he must have thought better of it. He turned his hands palm up.

'Come, there is much to learn.' The next minute he was striding out into the reception area. Sophie followed, her mind jumping at the unspoken words and the effort to keep up.

A heavy wooden door led to the back of the building. Jean-Luc pushed it wide for her and she stepped out, expecting to have to readjust her eyes to the glare of the day. Instead, she found herself in a cool, stone alleyway. Muted shafts of sunlight filtered in from each end of the alley, warming the brown stones.

'How well do you know Lyon, Sophie?'

'I visited a couple of times with my grandmother. Not really long enough to get to know it well.'

'Perhaps you've already seen a few alleyways like this one?'

Sophie nodded. She'd walked through Lyon's old town the day before, trying to familiarise herself with the city in the Sunday afternoon quiet. The alleyways that crisscrossed the town were almost ghostly in their stillness.

'This covered alleyway was built hundreds of years ago to keep the weavers' silk dry when it rains. Water can ruin silk. Lyon is full of alleyways like this. They even have a special name — we call them traboules. They were built especially to protect the rolls of silk from the rain. There was once a time when every traboule in Lyon was full of silk workers.'

Sophie's vivid imagination pictured the alleyways as they once must have been, full of the weavers and their brightly-coloured rolls of silk, cool channels of industry cutting through the city.

'It's a tragedy,' she said. 'All that history gone.'

'Yes, it is a tragedy.' Jean-Luc smiled at her ready sympathy. 'We have a saying that there are three rivers at the heart of Lyon. There's the river Rhône, the river Saône, and there's the river of tears left by the silk workers.' He looked back down the traboule, past the sombre stones to the motes of dust swirling in the sunshine beyond. 'Most of the mills in this city are closed. I intend to bring silks back to their rightful place in Lyon.'

His deep voice was filled with animation.

'You feel very passionately about this, don't you?' She looked at him, curious. She had wondered how a man who had such a dangerous, adrenaline-fuelled career could find fulfilment in this change of occupation. Now she watched his eyes deepen to a dark sea-blue and realised that he would bring the same passion to every area of his life.

'Yes, I do feel passion.' He raised his head proudly. 'I aim to keep the old traditions alive. Come with me and see.'

He was already striding towards the blue door of the weaving shed at the end of the alley. Sophie took quick steps to keep up with his long legs. An electronic keypad, a reminder of centuries of progress, allowed them entry at the push of a code. Jean-Luc slung the heavy door wide and stood back to let Sophie through. Inside, a deafening racket filled her ears. The contrast with the quiet alleyway could not have been greater. She brought her hands up to her head, then felt Jean-Luc's hand in the small of her back, propelling her forward. When she turned to look up at him, she realised he was laughing at her expression of dismay. The noise was too loud for her to hear him. He handed her some ear-protectors with a gesture for her to put them on.

Inside the high-ceilinged room were six large looms, each fast and furiously in operation. Jean-Luc guided her along a walkway past the weavers to a glass-fronted office at the end of the shed. The six loom operators, each wearing sturdy ear protection, turned to watch their progress. Each, in turn, lifted a hand in deferential greeting as Jean-Luc passed. The looms were working at tremendous speed, the threads whirling so fast from side to side it was almost impossible to see how they were propelled. A selection of jade and peacock-blue silks inched steadily upwards and out of the machines. Propped on racks along one wall were great cones of yarn in every imaginable hue. Jean-Luc pushed open the glass door of the office.

'*Bonjour*, M. Olivier.' A small, dark-haired woman greeted them from behind her desk. In the relative quiet of the sound-proofed office, Sophie removed her ear muffs whilst Jean-Luc made the introductions.

'Irina, I'd like to introduce Sophie, our student from England. Sophie, this is Irina, our supervisor here in the weaving-shed. Irina keeps our orders on track and our weavers in order.' Jean-Luc threw Irina a smile before turning to Sophie. 'If there's ever anything you need to know, Irina will be happy to help you.'

Irina stretched out her hand, her dark eyes flicking from Jean-Luc to Sophie. Sophie felt her swift assessment, but the older woman must have liked what she saw. She gave what appeared to be a small nod of approval before falling into an animated discussion with Jean-Luc about the peacock-blue fabric they were weaving. It was intended for the opening of an opera house in Italy, the date of which loomed ever nearer. In spite of the urgency, Jean-Luc was calm and decisive, and Irina, just like the designers and the young men operating the looms, showed him a very obvious respect.

It was a very thoughtful Sophie who

accompanied her boss back across the shadowy traboule to start her new job. Little was said between them during their short walk. Sophie was trying to accustom herself to this new Jean-Luc. He had told her he hadn't changed, that the man inside was still the same. Occasionally, she stole a glance at his profile. She remembered the strength of purpose that had been there when they first met. In that regard, Jean-Luc was most definitely the man she remembered.

But if it were really true that in every regard he was the same man he was four years ago, then Sophie had seriously underestimated him. The glamorous celebrity was revealing himself to be a man with far more depth than she had realised. One thing about him had certainly not changed, however — he still had the same incredibly powerful and persuasive personality. And Sophie realised with a chill that in one respect, she herself had not changed — she still felt the same dangerous attraction. If Jean-Luc decided to test her resolve, she wasn't sure how long it would take before she crumbled. The two months she was about to spend in Lyon was beginning to seem a very long time.

When Jean-Luc left her in front of the paperwork in her office, a fresh cup of coffee by her side, to return to his desk, Sophie was more than glad to have some breathing space and some time to make sense of her new world. She realised with a sinking feeling that the Jean-Luc she had come to know that morning was a force to be reckoned with. It was time to start building her defences.

*   *   *

Jean-Luc sat at his desk, his computer screen glowing bright with incoming emails and his mobile phone beeping insistently. He looked at them both for several seconds, switched them off, stood again restlessly, and moved towards the window. Outside, the morning was fast approaching noon, and the cars parked below shone in the glare of the sun. The baker in the pâtisserie opposite was arranging a display of pastries in his window. Shoppers bustled in and out of the doorway, clutching paper bags filled with brioches and croissants. The streets of Lyon were full of activity. Jean-Luc stared down, oblivious.

For the first time in his life, he felt himself at a stand, uncertain how to proceed. When Sophie left him so abruptly all those years ago, he had thought her as duplicitous and greedy as the rest of the groupies who surrounded him. But now it seemed he should have trusted his original instincts. From the time he met her again at her grandmother's funeral, he'd known the girl was an innocent. Everything about her proclaimed it. The way she moved, the way she spoke, the way he caught her assessing him gravely with those incredible violet eyes. And her assessment was not the calculation of a woman intent on making use of him. It was the assessment of a girl who was wary, and was biding her time until she had made up her mind about him.

He turned away from the window abruptly, running his fingers through his hair in an old gesture of uncertainty, one he hadn't used for years. He caught sight of the photo of his young, triumphant self on the wall and grimaced.

'Well, what about it?' he asked his younger self sternly. 'You think I'm a fool to trust her, don't you?' The old self in the photo smiled back in smug silence.

'Okay, maybe,' Jean-Luc conceded. 'But not such a fool as you were. You thought taking her to bed would be the answer.' Jean-Luc grunted his contempt for his reckless youth. 'Well, congratulations. Thanks to your hot-headedness, she ran away from you.'

He sat down and flicked his computer screen on, trying to concentrate.

The number of emails in his inbox had doubled. He stared at them blankly. All he could see was Sophie. Sophie looking a picture of innocent maturity in her pencil skirt, the swell of her curves deliciously attractive. She had grown up in a more delightful way than he could ever have imagined.

He flicked a last look over his shoulder at his younger self. 'This time we do things my way,' he said decisively. '*Doucement*. Patiently. There will be no more running away.'

His photo didn't respond. Jean-Luc turned his back and began pressing the keys on his computer mechanically.

* * *

For the first couple of weeks into her new job, it seemed Sophie had nothing to worry about. After that first morning, Jean-Luc was hardly present in the mill building, his drive to build up the business taking him out most days to visit potential customers and investors.

A couple of times he had raced in to see Charles, the accountant. Sophie passed him on one of these occasions as she came down the main staircase. He was flying towards her, mounting the stairs two by two, head down. There was rather a careworn look about him, but he raised his head on seeing her, and instantly a handsome smile dispelled his drawn features.

'Ça va, Sophie?' A hand reached up and brushed her cheek lightly. Then he was gone. Sophie watched his retreating figure leap up the stairs and lifted a hand to touch her cheek, her fingers moving over the spot where his own had been. She had found herself leaning into his caress as he passed, touched by the surprising gentleness of the gesture. Now, for a couple of seconds, she stood rooted to the spot. The past couple of weeks had seen the hard edges of her mistrust of Jean-Luc gradually begin to wear away. He had kept his distance, allowing her to settle in with her new work colleagues in her own time. But more than that, in his absence she had begun to realise just how seriously she had underestimated him. His entire staff, from the accountant to the youngest apprentice in the weaving-shed, spoke of him with the highest regard. This was not the shallow thrill-seeker she had once thought, but a man whose staff respected him, who showed a passionate drive and commitment to his workers. Within just two weeks, Sophie had been forced to dramatically revise her opinion of him. Jean-Luc Olivier was not like the others in her grandmother's circle.

She dropped her fingers from her cheek, head drooping. Jean-Luc might be a paragon to his staff, but he was still a dangerously persuasive man. And the thought that his will was so strong he might even have the power to make her forget herself, make her forget the promise she was intent on keeping, sent a chill through her.

She shivered and began her descent of the stairs. She might have been wrong in her judgement of Jean-Luc, but he was still a force to be reckoned with.

* ★ *

In Jean-Luc's absence the designers, Céline and Louisa, were fast becoming Sophie's friends, showing her the sights of La Croix-Rousse in their lunch hour and picking out the best shops and restaurants for her. Although she was still homesick, she was making friends in the student accommodation she was living in, too. The halls were noisy and her room poky, but the French students who shared the accommodation were friendly, and she had already declined several party invitations. She was able to tell her father and Jack almost truthfully that she was doing fine. But the real truth was, she was permanently on edge.

'Hey, Sophie,' Louisa called into her office one Friday afternoon. 'It's the weekend. What are you up to tonight?'

'Oh, nothing much. It's been a long week for me. A quiet night in.'

'No way.' Louisa stared at her in horror. 'It's Friday night. Céline and I are going to a bar in the old town. Why don't you come with us?'

'No, honestly, old age is creeping up on me,' she explained herself, grinning widely. 'Maybe next weekend.'

'Getting old? Yeah, right. What you need is a hot date. Let's see what we can set you up with next week.' Louisa patted her shoulder affectionately, and even Céline giggled. The girls kissed Sophie several times, Gallic fashion, and departed on a waft of perfume and much excited chatter.

After they'd gone, a soft, pleasant silence crept over the office. Sophie turned off the radio and settled down into her paperwork. The late afternoon light from the window slanted on her bent head as she concentrated. From time to time, a stray lock fell over her eyes, and she would push the heavy strands back from her forehead with one impatient hand, the bronze band she wore sliding up her arm. For a long while, the only sound in the office was the large old clock on the wall, ticking over the minutes.

'Are you alone?' The deep voice startled her in the silence. She jumped and whirled round.

Jean-Luc was leaning against the door, his arms folded, watching her.

'It's you,' she cried, her voice high-pitched. 'How long have you been there?' She realised how startled she sounded. Her pen had fallen onto the desk with a clatter. She picked it up and turned back to her work. 'I'm just finishing this email. The accountant is still here.'

'No. I've just sent Charles home, too. Come, Sophie, it's Friday night. We're the last here. Put your pen down — our customers won't run away over the weekend.' He moved away from the door and stretched wearily, the muscles on his shoulders straining against his blue cotton shirt. Sophie's eyes widened. She bent hastily to switch off her computer.

'What are you doing this evening?' He moved nearer. When Sophie straightened, she could see the stubble which cast a dark shadow across his face. His expression as he asked the question was nonchalant, but there was tension in the lines around his eyes. He looked weary. She was surprised by a sudden urge to reach up and smooth the lines away. Putting her hands down firmly by her sides, she curled her fingers into her palms.

'I haven't got anything planned. I was going to get an early night.'

'An early night?' He laughed quietly. 'Why don't you let me take you out?'

The question was soft and low and totally unexpected. He stepped a little closer. Now that her computer was switched off, the room was very quiet. In the silence that followed his question, dull sounds from the street outside floated up and through the window. Sophie's desk shifted as she leaned back against it.

'I don't bite.' Jean-Luc was smiling now, approaching her slowly. 'And I have good manners in polite company. I'd like to take you out tonight.'

Sophie reached a hand out in a half-hearted gesture to push him away.

'I don't think that's a good idea.'

He stilled. The lift to his mouth remained, but the warmth left his eyes, to be replaced by a kind of weariness. For a second, unbelievably, Sophie thought she saw his head bow in defeat. She almost reached out to him, touched by his expression, but then he took a step nearer, and she dropped her hand, unnerved.

'Why not?' His head was up now, and his regard was steady. The silence stretched between them whilst he waited for her to answer. Sophie drew in a breath.

'I don't understand . . . ' She drew herself together and straightened her stance, annoyed with herself for letting him get under her defences. 'I don't understand you. You said you didn't like me running away, and so you brought me to work for you. I'm here.' She spread her arms wide. 'Isn't that enough?'

'No.'

The baldness of his answer caused her to flinch.

'What, then?' She almost cried out the words. He stepped a little closer, narrowing the gap between them, and she forced herself to stand straight, holding his gaze with her own. As he neared, she noted again the signs of tension in the set of his shoulders and in the shadows beneath his eyes.

'I brought you here because I wanted you to get to know me. To know that I'm not a monster.'

'I already know that. I've worked here long enough and heard enough about you to discover that for myself.'

The warmth of his smile returned. 'Then where's the danger in getting to know one another better? It's just a meal together, that's all.' He spread his hands. 'In a few weeks' time, you will be going back to London. We may never have another opportunity.'

Sophie bit her lip, gazing into his face as though it could provide a clue, some indication of how she should respond. He waited patiently, the uncomplicated warmth of his expression the only indication she had. He was right. There was no harm in getting to know him before she left for home. Maybe she owed him that, for her misjudgement of him.

'Okay,' she said, unsmiling. The answer surprised them both. His eyes gleamed briefly and he stepped back.

'*Bon*. I'll pick you up at eight.' He was turning away to open the door for her when she stopped him, running after him quickly and catching his arm.

'No, don't. There's no need to pick me up. I'll meet you somewhere.'

Her fingers on his arm clutched at him, insistent. She realised how odd this must seem and dropped her hand quickly, but not before he had noticed the anxiety in her voice.

'Are you hiding a secret from me?'

His weary eyes were suddenly alert and alive to the tension in her gaze. She stepped back a little.

'What are you hiding, I wonder?' he asked curiously, releasing his hold on the door handle. Her face held a trace of strain. Just inside the collar of the lemon blouse she was wearing, the hint of a pulse could be seen beating.

'Nothing. It's not that, it's just . . . ' Her protest trailed away and she dropped her eyes from his insistent gaze. How to explain to him that she didn't want him calling at her student accommodation? The stupid lie she had told him about inheriting her grandmother's wealth was preying on her mind. How to explain her reasons for living in a cramped, noisy building? And, most of all, how to explain that being seen on the arm of the famous Jean-Luc Olivier would put an instant barrier between her and the other students in the hall, just as she was trying to settle in? All her years of experience told her that any hint she moved in different circles would cause jealousy and resentment amongst her less well-off peers. If she'd learnt anything in her short life, it was to keep her world and her grandmother's apart.

In the end, she shrugged helplessly. 'I'm not hiding anything. It's just that I don't want to put you to any trouble.'

The excuse sounded pathetically lame, even to her own ears. There was silence for a few long seconds. Jean-Luc came away from the door.

'What is it?' He searched her face and then shrugged tiredly. 'You still don't trust me, do you?'

There was such weariness in his expression that Sophie had to restrain herself from throwing herself into his arms. She turned away and busied herself putting her keys in her bag.

'It's not that I don't trust you. It's not a question of trust.'

'Then it must be something else. Tell me.'

She studied her set of keys wordlessly for a moment before bringing her head round to face him.

'Okay, I'll tell you. I don't want you coming to pick me up because it would make the other students jealous, and they'd think I thought I was too good for them,' she finally blurted out.

Jean-Luc stepped back, an incredulous look on his face. 'Jealous?'

'Yes, jealous. I'm not like the other women you go out with. When I was at school in London, I learnt never to mention the famous people I met at my grandmother's, or wear any of the designer clothes she gave me. You don't understand, it's a different world. If the other students see me with you, they'll think I consider myself out of their league, and that's when the snide comments will start. I can't afford to lose any more friends.'

Jean-Luc stopped in his tracks, a look of genuine surprise on his face. He continued to stare at her for a moment or two, surprise turning to compassion and then a brief flare of anger. 'You don't need friends like those, Sophie.'

Sophie took in all the confidence of his stance, the broad shoulders, the careless assumption that nothing and no one would get in his way, and wished she shared his strength.

'It's easy enough for you not to care what people say.' There was no bitterness in her tone, just a world-weary resignation. 'For you, everything is easy.'

'Is it? Perhaps I haven't had quite the easy life you imagine.' Sophie was struck by the sudden harshness in his tone. His eyes filled with the same bleakness she had seen in them when she had asked her careless question about his past. The impression was a fleeting one, barely registered. Before she could respond, he was carrying on in his usual determined way.

'I will pick you up at eight this evening.'

She opened her mouth to speak, but he raised his hand.

'As a compromise, this time I will wait for you outside. Suitably discreet.'

The smile on his lips reached his eyes, and when it did, Sophie knew her resistance was beaten.

'If you prefer, I'll wear aviator shades,' he continued. 'And a baseball cap.'

Her lips twitched against her will, her cheeks creasing into a smile.

'You don't like the baseball cap? Maybe a balaclava?' he suggested.

Sophie gave up, breaking into a giggle despite herself. 'Fine, I suppose you win. I don't seem to have much choice.'

As he began to retreat, satisfied, she stopped him with another question. 'Are you always this overbearing?'

'Overbearing?' For the first time, Sophie actually saw him look disconcerted. He gave a half-laugh. 'You really don't have a very high opinion of me, do you?'

'I think it's very difficult to stand up to you once you've made your mind up,' she said honestly.

There was a slight frown as he digested her words. But then he shrugged and smiled, and his eyes were full of their previous assurance. 'Come, it's time for you to go. Let me finish off here. I'll see you this evening.'

Sophie made her way home on the metro, too distracted to notice the usual Friday evening crush. The carriage was packed and she stood swaying in the aisle, hanging from a strap. Occasionally, a fellow commuter would stumble into her, but she just stared abstractedly at her reflection in the blackened window.

She knew that by accepting Jean-Luc's invitation, she was entering dangerous ground. She tried to work out where the road had started, but even if she could make it out, she didn't know how to turn back. It was like entering a marsh, where every footstep dragged her deeper and deeper down. At the end of the road, though, she knew she would be returning to London. The thought of her dad and brother was like a safety jacket.

Two months, and then she would be back in London and her other life. Then the comforting thought turned to taunting, and her treacherous mind kept asking her: was it so wrong to want to live in the present? To enjoy these two months to the full? She was filled with a restless excitement. The same wild sap of recklessness was rising up within her as had swept over her the night of her grandmother's party. With a supreme effort of will, she tried to stem the mounting tide, but as she exited from the metro station into the hot evening sun, a rush of adrenaline coursed through her. Jean-Luc had said they should take the opportunity to get to know each other better, and she had accepted his words. And now she would also have the chance to show him she was more than the Miss Moneypenny he had teased her with. And that she was no longer a teenage girl.

She swung her bag, feeling almost happy for the first time in months.

4

Once back in her student room, Sophie showered quickly, discarding her prim office outfit with relief. At home in London, she'd decided at the last minute to pack a few of the vintage designer dresses her grandmother had handed down to her over the years. She'd had no idea if there would be any occasion to wear them, but guessed she might as well be prepared. Now she blessed both her forethought and her grandmother's generosity. She rifled through the hangers, putting them under rapid inspection. She wanted something that would impress, that would show Jean-Luc she was a force to be reckoned with.

Her midnight-blue dress brushed past her fingers on the rail, the delicate silk fabric darkly gleaming. Her hand hovered for a moment, and then she lifted down the hanger. The material came alive, as she knew it would, soft as night in her hands. She shrugged herself into it, smoothing it over her figure like a glove. The long sleeves fitted tightly to her arms, reaching over her wrists, and the bodice clung softly to her curves, the high hem of the skirt revealing the length of her tanned legs. Puritanical and alluring. Sophie shivered as she gazed at her reflection. The last time she'd worn the dress had been at a family gathering. Safe enough. But alone with Jean-Luc?

Her violet eyes looked back at her from the mirror, gleaming with excitement, begging her not to back down. A heady recklessness continued to course through her veins, unstoppable. She reached for her make-up before her inner voice of caution could prevent her, pulling out a dramatic dark eye shadow and kohl eyeliner. When she had finished, her reflection smiled back in triumph. She lifted the tiny silver watch encircling her wrist. Time to go.

She picked up her bag with a hand that she noted was trembling a little, and stepped out into the corridor. All quiet.

She'd imagined the other students were out in the bars of Lyon, but it seemed not everyone had left yet. A handsome young man stepped out of the room opposite in a waft of aftershave, dressed to kill. He did a dramatic double-take and gave a long, appreciative whistle.

'Sugar, you're sure knocking them dead tonight. Who's the hot date?'

Sophie's neighbour had insisted on calling her Sugar ever since their first meeting in the student canteen. Whereas all the other girls had been wearing jeans and cotton shirts, he seemed to find her work outfits of pencil skirts and demure blouses amusing.

'It's not a date, Marco,' she said, pursing her lips primly. 'I'm going out with my boss.'

'Whoa.' Marco's eyebrows rose. 'He must be some boss.'

'Is it too much?' She dropped her

supercilious attitude and regarded him anxiously. Marco was studying fashion design and had an unerring eye. They were fast becoming friends, and she had a high regard for his opinion. Suddenly, his extravagant reaction made her feel incredibly self-conscious. Marco stepped back, his wide-eyed, ironic gaze sweeping slowly over her long, bare legs.

'Sugar, it's wa-a-ay too little,' he drawled eventually.

'Oh.' Her face fell, and she stared down at her own bare, sweeping legs in consternation. Then she glanced at her watch again. Five minutes past. Was there time to change?

'Don't even think about it.' Marco had read her mind. 'You look gorgeous. You keep that dress on.'

Sophie threw her friend a grateful look and turned to hurry down the corridor.

'You keep that dress on until your boss tells you it's time to take it off,' he called after her.

She turned back, scowling. 'Marco, I

told you it's not that sort of date.'

She had descended two flights of stairs before the inviting image Marco conjured up subsided.

Outside, the dying sunlight was still warm on the pavement. A handful of dust swirled in golden motes at her feet. There was a small pause as she adjusted her eyes from the darkness inside her building.

'*Bonsoir*, Sophie,' Jean-Luc's voice greeted her, low and deep. She stepped out from the doorway. He was leaning back against his car, his driver waiting patiently behind the wheel. As she approached, he straightened up, eyes widening.

'Where is Miss Moneypenny?'

She had unpinned her hair from the swept-up style she wore to work, leaving it to fall in thick lengths down her back. Jean-Luc let his gaze travel in stunned surprise down the length of her, lingering on the midnight blue of her silk dress, down the length of her bare, tanned legs to her slim, sandaled feet with a jewelled ankle chain.

For once, he appeared to have lost some of his iron control. Sophie's kohl-rimmed eyes gleamed. 'It's Friday,' she said softly. 'Miss Moneypenny has the night off. You'll have to take me instead.'

Jean-Luc drew in his breath sharply. Too late, she realised the double meaning. She threw him a quick glance. He was standing motionless, his eyes darkened to the same deep blue as her dress. To her horror, she saw he had two bands of dark colour staining his cheekbones.

'Come,' he said roughly. 'Let's go.'

He turned and opened the car door for her. Sophie stepped forward hesitantly. Dressing like this had been a stupid idea. She slid into the car, the leather seat cool against her bare legs, and turned to reach for her seat belt. Jean-Luc was still standing on the pavement, the door wide, his gaze fixed hotly on the top of her legs, where the dramatic blue silk of her dress skimmed her thighs. Then the door slammed closed.

Sophie's hands shook a little as she tried to fix her belt. She had meant to show Jean-Luc she had matured, that she was in control. Within an instant of seeing him, she was plunged out of her depth. Way, way out of her depth.

The other door swung wide, and then he was sitting next to her, his lean hand resting lightly on the seat beside her bare legs. Then the driver turned the ignition and the car swung lightly into the dwindling traffic. Sophie turned her head to the window, avoiding Jean-Luc's gaze. It had been a mistake to come. She seemed to be making lots of mistakes recently, she conceded miserably.

As if guessing her thoughts, Jean-Luc reached out one hand to lift hers in a light grasp.

'I told you you could trust me,' he said, his deep voice steady. He caught up her hand and brought it, intertwined in his fingers, to rest between them.

Their bodies were acres apart on the leather seat. It was a gesture of reassurance, nothing more. Nevertheless, Sophie felt the warmth of his hand seep upwards like warm honey through her veins. She felt his thumb brush her wrist and knew that, after all, she did trust him.

It was herself she didn't trust.

* * *

The restaurant Jean-Luc took her to was in the snug old town on the other side of Lyon's two wide rivers. A quietness had fallen over them during the drive, and they took their seats without speaking in a softly-lit corner of the room. Sophie cast a quick glance in Jean-Luc's direction, wondering if he felt the same tension she did, but his handsome face was, as ever, unreadable. He passed her one of the leather-bound menus on the table.

One of the waiters lit their candles. His arm moved past her to shift the centrepiece slightly, but when Sophie looked up from her menu to thank him, the waiter studiously avoided her eye. Looking from the discreet waiter back to Jean-Luc, she raised an eyebrow, putting two and two together.

'So, do you come here often?' she asked, her nerves making her voice more brittle than she intended.

'It's one of my favourite restaurants, yes.'

'I thought so. Very discreet.'

Jean-Luc didn't reply. When Sophie looked up, she found him regarding her with some amusement.

'There aren't many places I can go without being asked for my autograph. But I think you're asking me if I often bring other women here?'

She glowered. Did he have to know every single thing she was thinking? 'Yes, that's what I meant. You're very sharp, aren't you? No flies on you.'

'What? What do you mean, flies?' he asked incredulously, looking over both shoulders, as though expecting a cloud of bluebottles to be hovering over him.

'Yes, flies. It's an English idiom: 'There are no flies on you'. It means no one can make a fool of you.'

'Flies,' he repeated seriously. 'No flies on me.' He kept his steady gaze on hers with all the appearance of solemnity, but there was a tell-tale twitch in his cheek. Eventually his blue eyes lit up, and he began to laugh out loud. Sophie realised how ridiculous the expression must sound and, in spite of herself, relaxed into a giggle.

'It's true. I know it sounds silly, but that's what people say.'

'Only the English could have such a saying,' he teased.

'*Bien*, bah.' She lifted her shoulders in a Gallic shrug. 'As you French say, *vive la différence*.'

'Let's drink to that, *chérie*.' He turned to bring one of the silent waiters hurrying over. Sophie bent her head to her menu. When she heard Jean-Luc give his order, and the heavy menu snap shut in his strong hands, she looked up, the smile still on her lips.

'That's better.' Jean-Luc's eyes gleamed. 'You look very beautiful when you smile.'

In an instant, her happiness was gone. Her face was a mask of wariness.

'No, don't look at me like that again, *chérie*. It's true, and I mean what I say. You don't smile often enough.'

His tone was quite serious. Sophie realised he meant it. She didn't smile often enough. It was true: she hadn't smiled much since her mother died. Then her father's health and money worries, and making sure there was enough for her brother's music lessons . . . If it weren't for the promise she'd made her mother — a promise she fulfilled with heroic desperation — she would have broken down long ago. And then her grandmother's death, on top of everything. Sometimes it seemed as though a big, black cloud of misery was following her everywhere she went. She knew she had a reputation at college for being buttoned up. And now apparently she didn't smile often enough. Well, sometimes it was hard to find reasons to smile.

To her horror, she felt ready tears spring to her eyes. She bent her head quickly, pretending to study her menu, but Jean-Luc reached his hand out and gently lifted her chin.

'Look at me, Sophie.'

'I'd better not,' she said, keeping her eyes down.

He was silent for a moment, his hand warm under her chin. Then he released his grip and reached into his pocket.

'Here, this is the second handkerchief you've had from me.' He pressed a freshly-ironed handkerchief into her hand. 'Are you starting a collection?'

Sophie did look up then and briefly showed one of her precious smiles. She blew her nose. 'Yes, well, I need something to keep me occupied in the long evenings. And it beats stamps.'

He chuckled. 'That's better. You know, I'm beginning to realise you have a lot of spirit. But it's not good to keep it all bottled up.' He took the menu from in front of her. 'Why don't I choose you something good from this menu, and while we're eating, you can unburden yourself. What's that other English saying? 'A problem shared is a problem halved'?'

A look of amazement crossed Sophie's face. No one ever said this sort of thing to her. 'Is this for real? How lovely that sounds. Just talk to someone and your problems are gone — *pouf.*' She snapped her fingers. 'Like that.'

'Try it. It might just be as easy as that. You know, I have very broad shoulders.' He smiled again. Sophie noticed, not for the first time, that he really did have broad shoulders. And a dangerously attractive smile.

His eyes had darkened to a smoky blue in the candlelight. She imagined a world where she could drown helplessly in those eyes, where there would be no waking up, no cold realisation of the gulf between them, no return to her drab life and her incessant worries. A world where the famous Jean-Luc

Olivier could come home to her housing estate on Foxglove Road, and sit in the local pub with Jack and her dad like normal people. And newspapers wouldn't be taking photos of her and her family, and asking what Jean-Luc Olivier was doing with little Sophie from the estate when he used to go out with film stars. And no one would be saying she was chasing him for his money, like they did when Louis came.

Yeah, right. And then her fairy godmother would wave a wand and she'd have a golden carriage to go home in.

It was fortunate for Jean-Luc that just at that moment the waiter came to take their order, because Sophie's train of thought had brought her back to where they'd started — at her eighteenth birthday party in Paris. A hard knot formed in her chest as she remembered the rumours going round that night: Sophie Challoner was an English Cinderella, on the prowl to catch a rich husband. Well, it wasn't true. She didn't need a rich husband or Jean-Luc or anyone else. Then the silly lie she'd told him about being her grandmother's heiress came to mind, and her spirits sank even further. She had lied to him, and it made her feel bad. What a tangled web.

She looked over to where Jean-Luc was going through the menu, his handsome features sepia-warm in the candlelight. Well, in any case, there was no point thinking like this. In a few weeks' time, Cinderella's party would be well and truly over. She would be able to forget all about dating Jean-Luc Olivier and go back to Foxglove Road. And then she would be able to live happily ever after, she thought dismally.

The waiter moved away from the table, and Sophie raised her head to find Jean-Luc's quizzical gaze resting on her.

'Lost in thought,' he said.

She forced a smile. 'I'm sorry. It's good of you to order for me.'

'No problem.' He bowed his head. 'And you're right,' he said, carrying on their previous conversation, 'I have brought other women to this restaurant. But none of them seem to share your reluctance for my company.'

Sophie started, horrified at appearing so rude, but Jean-Luc merely held up a hand. There was a self-mocking twist to his mouth.

'Don't worry,' he said. 'Maybe it will do me good. I'm beginning to think the next few weeks in your company will be a salutary experience.'

An awkward silence fell. Sophie was wondering if Jean-Luc were beginning to regret his invitation.

'How is your family?' he prompted, breaking the silence. 'Is your father well?'

'Oh, Dad . . . ' It was the wrong question. Sophie's blue eyes clouded over. To her disgust, she felt her treacherous chin wobble again.

What was it about Jean-Luc that made her feel so incredibly vulnerable?

She was used to hiding her problems under her veneer of aloofness, but he insisted on bringing everything into the open. She took a fortifying gulp of wine, hoping it wasn't an expensive bottle. For all the attention she was paying it, it might as well have been lemonade.

'My dad hasn't been well,' she said, her voice reasonably controlled. 'After my mother died, he had a breakdown. He had a business restoring antiques, but he wasn't able to pay it much attention during my mother's illness. Debts built up. Then the business failed, too.'

'So you left school to earn some money,' Jean-Luc finished for her. He was watching her intently. She had been gazing into the distance, but at his question she refocused sharply.

'Yes, that's right,' she said, a little too crisply.

'Things must have been hard.' His tone was unusually gentle. Dangerously so.

Sophie felt all the danger inherent in confiding in him and made her reply deliberately dismissive. She was sick and tired of being constantly reminded of the difference between their situations, but every topic of conversation seemed to lead back to one thing. 'We managed okay. As you said yourself, I was earning good money.'

Jean-Luc refilled her wine glass patiently and tried again. 'And how about your brother? How did he cope when your mother died?'

'Jack?' She softened immediately. 'He took it hard. But he's very strong. Stronger than I am in many ways.'

Jean-Luc raised an eyebrow, as though such a thing were impossible.

'It's true, really.' Sophie laughed, and Jean-Luc's hand stilled on his wine glass as she leaned forward, full of unguarded affection for her brother. She lifted her eyes to his. 'Jack has a brilliant gift for music. He's played the violin since he was six. But when Mum died, music saved his life. He played for hours and hours and hours on end in his room. It was as though the music reached him in a way that Dad and I couldn't.'

She felt the betraying tears prickle again. Jean-Luc reached out to where her hand lay clenched on the tabletop and uncurled her fingers gently in his own.

'It must have been a comfort to him, having a gift like that.'

'Yes.' Her mouth lifted in something like half a smile, but the sadness was still there. 'His teacher used to tell me he played like an angel possessed.'

'I'd love to hear him sometime.'

Instantly she withdrew her hand. The waiter approached their table bearing two steaming plates, and she took refuge from his questions in the arrival of their meal.

'Oh, thank you. I didn't think I was hungry. This looks delicious.'

Sophie tucked in heartily, her plate piled with all the Lyonnais delicacies he had chosen for her. From time to time, he took a sip from his wine glass, and occasionally she felt his speculative gaze resting on her bent head.

By the time Jean-Luc had chosen her dessert, a deliciously crunchy *tarte aux pralines*, Sophie felt she had opened up more than she had to anyone since her mother died. She stole a look at his strong features and felt a twinge of guilt. He had been a patient listener. But if she told him the truth — the real truth, about the debts that still awaited her when she returned to London — what then? The balance of power, already weighted in favour of Jean-Luc, would shift entirely in his direction. At least, whilst he thought she had money of her own, she had a hope of meeting him on equal territory.

And underlying it all was the fear of succumbing to his strength of will. She needed to remain focused on her goal, to complete her studies and return to caring for her family. No matter how much temptation Jean-Luc threw in her way, she mustn't allow him to cause her to waver.

Breaking into her train of thought, Jean-Luc spoke again. 'Your grandmother is nothing like your father and brother. You must have felt very out of place with her circle of friends.'

'Yes, I did,' she agreed. 'And my mother hated it. She was happy to leave Paris to be with my dad. But I always felt a little sorry for my grandmother. She was very lonely underneath it all.' Sophie's eyes filled with a sudden fierce light. 'Anyway, I had to keep up my visits to her. When Mum died, I promised her I'd look after everybody.'

Jean-Luc stilled in the act of pouring more wine. Sophie was placing her dessert spoon beside her empty bowl, oblivious to his attention. He replaced the bottle gently on the table.

'That must have been a heavy burden on such young shoulders.' His blue eyes met hers steadily.

Sophie had never thought of it as a burden. She'd made a promise, and

114

carrying out that promise had become as natural to her as living and breathing. There was just that one time when she'd slipped . . . Just once, when she'd thought with despair of the blow life had dealt her. If only she'd been able to stay, four years ago, and forget her promise. She imagined staying, spending another night with Jean-Luc, and then another; all the nights they could have spent together. The thought of such unimaginable happiness was too much for her. Intense regret passed through her. Her voice was hollow when she answered.

'Sometimes it's been hard,' she said, 'but things have been getting easier over time.'

'Of course. Your grandmother's inheritance must have helped your family.'

She flicked her head up with a quick gesture, then changed the subject abruptly.

'What about you?' she asked. 'Do your parents live in Lyon?'

'No, my father left us when I was a

baby. He's in the States somewhere. We speak from time to time. My mother died three years ago.'

'Oh.' She raised her face then, her eyes gentled with sympathy, but the expression that met hers was cold and empty. She felt a sudden shock as though she had been rebuffed. It was as if, with the mention of his personal life, the portcullis had come down and he had retreated behind a high wall. She stared at him for a moment, perplexed. He didn't expand on his bald, factual story. His blue eyes were chilly.

'I'm sorry,' she said simply.

The coldness left him. He smiled in response, and immediately the barrier lifted. His features were filled with a delicious warmth. Sophie felt the familiar tug deep inside and, despite herself, allowed her eyes to linger hungrily on that mobile mouth, revelling in the luxury of sensation. When his lips stilled, she forced her gaze upwards to meet his and found him staring at her with an intensity that matched her own, his eyes darkened to a ferocious blue. For a long moment, she was incapable of movement. He shifted slightly, and she retreated, but too late. The gulf between them had been breached.

Sophie faltered back from the brink. 'I've told you about myself, but I — I don't know anything about you.'

She tried to keep the note of alarm out of her voice, but suddenly she felt as though she had been outwitted in a game of strip poker. She had been laying herself bare, whilst all the time Jean-Luc was fully clothed.

'You can easily find out about me. Google my name.' His deep voice was bored. The warmth had gone from his smile again.

He lifted his hand to the ever-vigilant waiter and asked him to bring them coffees and cognac. When he turned back, he looked surprised by the change in Sophie's expression.

'You want me to look you up on the internet?' she asked in disgust. 'I'm not interested in how often you won the World Championship or the make of car you drove.'

'Really? How demoralising.' He raised one well-defined eyebrow in faint surprise. 'And I thought I could be so proud of my achievements.'

'Yes, well,' she flustered. 'I'm sure you can . . . '

'Thank you.' He bowed graciously.

'But that's not the point.'

Jean-Luc smiled. 'I tell you what,' he said, his head tilted to one side as he eyed her pleasantly. 'You answer one more question of mine, and then I'll answer any questions of yours you want. No holds barred.'

Maybe if Sophie hadn't drunk the wine, she wouldn't have been so relaxed. Maybe her wits would have been sharper. As it was, her answer came totally unguarded.

'Okay, I agree.' She sank back into her chair, brows lifted. 'What's your question?'

Jean-Luc leaned forward slowly, the

smile gone from his face. With a shock, Sophie saw all trace of amiability leave him. His eyes were hard as sapphires.

'I've asked you this question once,' he said, the words travelling low and swift over the table between them. 'And you didn't answer. Four years ago you left me alone in a hotel room. Why?'

Sophie gasped. 'That's not a fair question.'

The vehemence in her voice caused the waiter to jump and the coffee cups to rattle in his hands. He cast a quick, startled glance in Sophie's direction before pushing the coffee hurriedly into place. Sophie sat up straight in her chair.

'And, actually, I prefer not to talk about the past,' she said. The tone of her voice held a glacial iciness. Her brother Jack would have known straight away it was pointless continuing the conversation. Jean-Luc, as she was fast coming to realise, was not so easy to manipulate.

'I think my question is perfectly fair.'

He spoke mildly, but there was no escaping the steel in his voice. 'And, more than that, I think you owe me an explanation.'

'I don't owe you anything.' Sophie picked up her cognac and took a gulp that left her spluttering. Her undignified choking failed to move him. He waited until she had finished and then continued implacably, his eyes never wavering from hers.

'I don't agree. That night you seduced me. You pretended to be experienced, a groupie even, and all the time you were a virgin.'

'Keep your voice down,' Sophie hissed, looking round anxiously at the nearby diners. Her face flamed scarlet, the bright blush a dead giveaway. 'And anyway, I did not seduce you.'

'I'm right, aren't I? You were a virgin.' His eyes narrowed to dazzling slits. 'Do you think it's a nice feeling, to be made use of?'

'I wasn't making use of you,' Sophie protested.

And then it finally hit her. With a shock of belated realisation, she finally understood how Jean-Luc must have construed the events of that night. She stared horror-struck into his piercing gaze. Then her cheeks began a slow burn of mortification. He must have thought she'd had a one-night stand to lose her virginity with a celebrity. When she remembered that she'd told him afterwards she was engaged, too, she hung her head. What must he have thought of her?

'That's not how it was,' she whispered. She twisted her napkin in her lap. She hadn't thought he would find their night together important. His previous girlfriends were so glamorous, she thought she'd be just another one on the list, soon to be forgotten.

She lifted her eyes to his. 'It wasn't how it seemed. I didn't think . . . '

The coldness in his expression brought her to a halt.

'You didn't think,' he echoed, with an icy quiet. 'You didn't think that I might actually have a heart. That I might care.'

Sophie looked down at the creased napkin, a sick feeling in the pit of her stomach. There was nothing she could say. It was true. She hadn't thought he'd care. In fact, she'd assumed him incapable of feeling. She'd thought he was as heartless as the hangers-on who surrounded him. When she dared to raise her eyes again, she found Jean-Luc hadn't moved an inch. His eyes had never left her, their hardness unyielding.

She pushed her untouched coffee away.

'I'd like to go home now,' she said quietly. Her request sounded childish, even to her own ears, but she could no longer endure his justified anger. He continued to look at her for several long seconds. Then he shrugged.

'Very well. I will call for my car. But understand this: I'm not asking you for an apology. I'm asking you for an explanation. And you still haven't answered my question — so we will continue this discussion on the way home.'

'Oh no, I . . . ' Sophie half-rose out of her seat, but her protest came too late. Jean-Luc had pushed back his chair and was already striding to the lobby, mobile phone in hand, to make his call. The waiters hurried to the table and began silently clearing away. Sophie looked so miserable that, for once, they forgot all attempts at discretion and were staring at her with open sympathy. Her bent head was still fixed on the napkin in her lap. How to tell Jean-Luc that she had run away because otherwise she would have felt bound to him, caught up in his iron will with no chance of escape? She had made a sacred promise to her mother to look after her father and brother. She had to leave him; there was no other choice. There was no way she could ever combine her world with his. The looks the waiters threw her were full of compassion, but it was no use. Sophie had guessed how it would be if she came to Lyon to work for him. For the first couple of weeks he had left her alone, lulled her into a false sense of security with his distance. But now he had removed the mask of indifferent charm to reveal the iron purpose she should have known all along lay underneath. This time there would be no getting away. Sophie put her head in her hands and wished the ground would open wide.

5

The heat of the day had turned cool when they stepped outside to the waiting car. Night had fallen. Jean-Luc held the car door for her wordlessly. Sophie slid inside, edging her way along the cool leather to the further corner. As she reached to click her seat belt in place, she felt Jean-Luc slide into the seat beside her. He turned, and their eyes met. What Sophie saw there dissolved her anxiety in an instant, and she drew in her breath in an unexpected rush of compassion. All the anger he had displayed inside the restaurant had left him. She was struck by the hollowness in his eyes on hers. Impulsively, she reached forward to catch both his hands in hers.

'I'm sorry,' she said, the words tumbling out of her rapidly. 'I didn't realise . . . If I could take that night back, I would.'

'Take it back?' His hands tightened fiercely on hers, his tone incredulous. 'Sophie — '

Before she could react, before she even guessed his intention, Jean-Luc pulled her toward him with the sweep of one powerful arm. Her breath left her body in a small gasp. With his other hand he swept her chin up to meet him, and then his lips were on hers. In an instant she was responding with an urgency of her own. He was holding her to him with all the force in his powerful arms, her body so tight against his chest she could feel the violent thudding of his heart against her ribcage.

Dimly, she registered the car was moving. Her senses filled with the warmth of him, the urgent heat of his mouth exploring hers. With no thought of breaking free, she reached up one hand to circle it around his strong neck, leaning in towards him, pulling him closer. Her gentle, passionate response

126

brought Jean-Luc to his senses. He pulled himself away, muttering under his breath. Sophie felt the grip of his hands on her shoulders as he pushed her at arm's length, the force in him eating into her so that she felt like a rag doll under his grasp.

'What is it?' Her breathing was uneven. She tried to regulate it, to sit up straight, but was powerless to move. She saw the direction of his gaze fall on her long bare legs as she twisted herself under the strength of his grip. With a curse, he dropped his hands from her shoulders and ripped his gaze away, so that now all she could see was his stark profile.

'Sophie,' he began again huskily. 'Sophie, this is not what I want.'

'Isn't it?' In that moment, a hollowness rushed to fill her, so that she could barely bring herself to speak. She turned her own face away in bewilderment. Outside the window, the black waters of the river Rhône could be seen as they crossed the bridge, orange lights bobbing and rippling on its surface. She let her curtain of hair swing forward to hide the misery in her expression and pressed her forehead unseeing to the glass. She felt Jean-Luc move to take her hand, his fingers gentle now, the strength in them subdued.

'This mustn't end the way it did before,' he said gently. 'We need to know each other better. I don't want you to run away again.'

Sophie said nothing. For a few moments, there was a deep, ominous silence. The timeless silence that falls before the surge of a tidal wave, before the swell reaches its peak to come crashing down blindly on the rocks.

Then an unstoppable anger surged through her. She whirled her head round.

'You think we need to get to know each other better?'

Jean-Luc reached one hand up to touch her face, taken aback by what he saw there, but she jerked back.

'What does that mean? I don't know

you at all,' she cried. 'All I know is, everything you set your heart on, you get. First of all, you railroad me into coming to work for you. Then when I get here, you talk me into going out with you, and you ask me all about myself, and you say nothing about you. And you insist on bringing up that night when I'm trying to forget all about it. And then I want you to kiss me, and you tell me you're not going to kiss me, like what I have to say doesn't mean anything!'

The rush of jumbled words left Sophie panting for breath, her face up close to Jean-Luc's in anger. He began to speak, but she broke in before the words could leave his mouth.

'I'm glad I left you in that hotel room, because you deserved it.' She jabbed one finger at his chest in violent confirmation. 'And I'm sorry I apologised before because, actually, I'm not sorry.'

Her final sentence spilled out incoherently, but she was beyond caring.

For a few moments, the only sound in the astonished silence was her rapid breathing as she forced for mastery of herself. She sank back again into her own corner, still not beaten.

'You're completely single-minded,' she added bitterly. 'And if it's any consolation, I've never known anyone like you.'

Her anger was stoked still further by Jean-Luc's reaction. In the half-light of the car, the street lamps lit up his face one after another in a regular pattern.

'Are you smiling?' she asked incredulously.

'I'm sorry I made you angry,' he said gently. 'When I want something, I don't always see what's in my way.'

'No, I've noticed. You're like a dog with a bone!'

'A dog with a bone?' he repeated, and now the smile on his face was unmistakeable. 'Is that a dog with no flies on him?'

'Oh, you're impossible.' Sophie snatched her hand out of his grasp and turned her face towards the window.

Jean-Luc drew back to his own side of the car and watched her crumpled figure in silence for a few moments. When he saw her hitch up one shoulder and shift even further away from him, his thoughts turned uncomfortably over her anger.

So she wanted him to kiss her. He wanted it, too, and wanted her. His body burned to reach for her, to pull her into his arms. For a split second, he wondered how it would be if he told his driver to change direction, to drive him to his apartment, where he could satisfy his hunger and make her his own. But it was a fleeting thought, quickly banished. He knew it would not make her his. She would be running again in the morning, and he would have lost her a second time.

Whatever barrier she had erected against him, he needed to understand it. And perhaps she was right; perhaps withholding himself was egotistical, too. God knew he had kept enough secrets in his life. He couldn't expect her to trust him if he continued to conceal them from her.

He watched her as the orange streetlamps played over her bent head. He knew she distrusted him, was rebelling at his attempts to take control, but the idea of letting their relationship play out in any other way, of it sliding out of his iron grasp, was too terrifying for him to contemplate.

From time to time, and always at moments of high tension, Jean-Luc was subject to brief, intense flashbacks to his painful history. Now, suddenly, a vivid image of his mother lying collapsed, half-comatose, on the floor of their house in Paris, came from nowhere to pierce his mind. So powerful a picture was it, his mouth went dry. He felt again the terrifying sensation of a world beyond his control and closed his eyes.

'It's not true that I always get what I want.'

His words brought Sophie's head up

slightly, as his previous assurance had failed to do. She considered his claim for several seconds then shrugged, unconvinced.

'So, you don't get what you want? The racing trophies, the fame and money, the glamorous women. Haven't you got what you wanted? What else is left?'

Jean-Luc had wrested control over his memories, and his mind was now firmly in the present. His voice was perfectly steady when he answered. 'Success isn't always measured by fame and money. And there is a lot left. You, for instance.'

At last her head turned towards him.

'Four years ago you ran away,' he continued softly. 'I didn't get what I wanted then.'

She stared at him wide-eyed. The car had finally reached her apartment block, preventing any reply. She uncurled herself from her tense position and stretched her long legs out in front of her.

'I'll see you to your door,' Jean-Luc said. He was out of the car and opening her door before she could protest. She climbed slowly out of her seat, and he kept his gaze resolutely averted as her long legs swung onto the pavement.

'Thank you for the evening,' she said stiffly. She hesitated a moment, her eyes levelled at some point on his shirt front. 'I'm sorry I lost my temper.'

He gave a quiet laugh.

'I love your apologies, *chérie*.' He stepped forward and took her hand in his, pulling her gently towards him. 'But it's not you who should be sorry. What are you doing next weekend?'

The abrupt question had her eyes instantly on his, narrowed and full of suspicion.

He laughed again. 'It's not a trick question. You said you didn't know me. If you like, I can take you out for the day, somewhere where you can get to know me better.'

'Where?' she asked suspiciously.

'You'll find out. Is it yes or no?' He

stepped even closer. 'The choice is yours.'

Sophie guessed that, after witnessing her anger, Jean-Luc was trying hard to let her be the one to make the decision, to let her be in control, for once. The trouble was, the insistence in his eyes and the dominance in his stance were totally at odds with his words. The difference was so great that in spite of the tensions of the evening, she was forced to hide a smile.

'And if I say no?' she asked.

For a moment, his eyes flamed with disappointment. He bit his lip with the effort of restraint. 'Then I will accept your decision.'

She tilted her head in disbelief. 'And then you will spend the rest of this week trying to persuade me.'

He laughed and held up his hands in surrender. 'Is it yes or no?' he repeated.

'I'll think about it.'

He bowed his head in reluctant acceptance.

A fresh night breeze whipped round

them, and Sophie shivered.

'Let yourself inside,' Jean-Luc said finally. 'It's getting cold.'

He waited until she had closed the glass doors behind her before lifting his hand in a small, brief wave. Then he ducked inside his car again, and the driver pulled away. Sophie watched through the glass as the vehicle disappeared, the indicators blinking orange, off and on, as it turned the corner. Then the street was empty.

★ ★ ★

A small lamp lit up Sophie's bedroom when she flicked it on, dispersing the shadows. The noise of people talking in the room below filtered upwards. Sophie fell onto her narrow bed and covered her face with one arm, trying to blot out the sound. If she really had inherited money from her grand-mother, as Jean-Luc thought, she would be living in a quiet flat in the suburbs; not here, in her spartan, noisy room.

She remembered how he had goaded her into the lie and felt a stab of guilt. She knew he no longer thought of her as a gold-digger. But somehow now, more than ever, she was frightened of showing him any sign of weakness. The evening had proved it. Jean-Luc was getting close, dangerously close. At the end of her placement, in a little under two months, she would have to summon up the resolve to leave him a second time, to go home to her father and Jack. She already knew how hard Jean-Luc would make it for her. And if there were the smallest chink in her armour . . .

Her mobile phone trilled once softly, interrupting her dark thoughts. The panel lit up with her brother's name. It was a sobering reality check. She knew Jack would never phone this late unless he had something important to say. The evening with Jean-Luc already had an unreal feel to it, like a dream from which she had just awakened. Just now real life was coming back to hit her with a massive thump.

'Hi, Soph, how's it going?'

'Fine. Everything alright with you? How's Dad?'

There was silence at the end of the line. Sophie could hear the faint sound of her brother's classical CD playing in the background and the click of a latch.

'Jack?' She tried to keep the anxiety out of her voice.

'It's okay. Just shutting the bedroom door. Dad's hovering.'

'Is he alright?'

'Not sure. Had a couple of letters this week that seemed to throw him a little. He went out yesterday in a suit and tie, and when he came back, he seemed a little agitated. Wouldn't tell me where he'd been.'

'Oh no. That's not good. Not good at all.' Sophie chewed her lip anxiously. Her father had had a total mental collapse after their mother died, but for the past few months, he had seemed to be on the road to recovery. This was a worrying setback. 'Do you think it could be the bank? But I paid off the last of the mortgage last year. I made sure it was clear before starting my course.'

'I know. But listen, I'm not saying this for you to worry about it. I just wondered if you knew what could be stressing him?'

'No. Should I come home, do you think? I could come back for the weekend.' Even as she said the words, Sophie was rapidly calculating the cost of a trip home, and her heart sank.

'I'll keep an eye on him, don't worry.' Her brother knew what she was thinking and was a step ahead of her. 'There's no need for you to waste money on the trip.'

Sophie registered, not for the first time, the new note of maturity in Jack's voice and was relieved to feel that she could rely on him.

'Okay,' she conceded reluctantly. 'But let me know if anything happens, won't you?'

'Course. Things will be fine. Anyway,

hey, guess what?'

'What?' she countered, amused at the excitement in Jack's voice.

'I've reached the final of the soloists' competition.'

'Wow, really, Jack?' Sophie was genuinely thrilled. She knew how hard he'd been practising. This was a prestigious national competition. No wonder he sounded so excited. 'I'm so happy for you.'

'Well, I won't let you down. Not after everything you've been through to pay for my lessons.'

There was a silence.

'You're not crying, are you?' Jack asked suspiciously.

'No, of course not.' Sophie sniffed loudly. 'I'm just really happy for you.'

'Oh, well, alright then. Listen, I'd better go before Dad comes in. Hope everything's okay with you?'

'Oh yes, just fine,' she replied breezily, still sniffing.

'That's good, then. Stay out of trouble.' Jack always laughed when he said goodbye to her this way. He found it amusing to think that sensible, reliable Sophie might do anything at all that would get her into trouble. At the moment, Sophie was struggling to think of the funny side.

* * *

That Saturday afternoon, another heat-filled day, found Sophie sitting at her desk in her student room, trying to concentrate on the college work in front of her. She had drawn her blinds against the sun. A large fan was blowing in one corner, shifting the hot air a few feet from side to side. She was just reading the same paragraph for the fourth time when there was a knock at the door.

'Hey, Sugar.'

'Come in, Marco,' Sophie answered in a long-suffering voice. She liked her student neighbour; but, like her brother Jack, he often teased her for being too serious. When he saw her at her desk, a spasm crossed his face.

'What are you doing? Working?' He flopped down on her bed in disgust. 'Do you want to see a film tonight? My tutor's asked me to do a project on 1940s fashion, and they're showing *Casablanca* in town.'

'*Casablanca?* Great,' she said, without looking up. 'Two star-crossed lovers meet in Paris and find that, actually, love doesn't conquer everything. That should really cheer me up.'

'Hmm. So the hot date with the boss didn't go too well, huh?'

'I told you it wasn't a date,' she said crossly.

'Whatever. Anyway, forget macho man, Sugar. You're too good for him, whoever he is. The film starts at eight. See you later.'

As it turned out, Sophie was glad of the distraction, since otherwise she would only have spent the evening brooding in her room. And Marco was excellent company. After the film, they walked through the city

142

companionably, carrying a fast food takeaway.

'Who'd have thought we'd resort to eating burgers in Lyon, the cuisine capital of France?' Sophie said, spearing a French fry into her ketchup.

Marco sighed. 'Yeah, well. Needs must on a student grant. Some of us don't get taken out to the best restaurants.'

'Come off it, Marco.' Sophie looked at his morose profile and laughed out loud. 'You love fast food.'

Suddenly, her laughter stopped abruptly, her footsteps slowing to a halt. Marco looked up to see what was troubling her and found she was watching a couple leave a hotel on the other side of the road. A blonde woman in a stunning gold evening dress was clutching the arm of the man beside her, and reaching up with her other hand to pat his broad chest possessively. One of the doormen raced down the carpeted steps to open the door of their car for them. Obviously some swanky party, judging by the line of limousines. Although the woman was striking, Marco's eyes were inevitably drawn to the man beside her, an imposing figure in his tuxedo. At first glance, they appeared to be the perfect alpha couple. Yet Marco guessed from the gentleman's constrained manner that he wasn't happy. Sure enough, when they reached the car, he firmly removed his companion's hand from its grasp on his elbow. As he did so, he lifted his head. His gaze found Marco's and held it indifferently. Marco frowned. He knew this man from somewhere, but couldn't place him.

Sophie stiffened beside him. Like a laser, the man caught her movement, his eyes sharpening in a flash from casual indifference to full mental alertness. He stepped away from the waiting car. The woman beside him clutched again at his elbow. Marco watched as she reached up to whisper something in his ear. There was no mistaking the look of disdain she had flashed in their direction.

Sophie was unnaturally still. Marco flicked his quick gaze to her bent head. She looked as though someone had punched her in the stomach. That settled it. He didn't know what was going on, but something prompted him to reach one well-manicured hand around her shoulder and pull her to him. It was an exaggerated display of affection, meant to challenge. The man in the tux went rigid, the hand at his side clenching into a fist. Marco stared back at him in slightly fearful defiance.

'I'd offer to go and punch him, but I think he's out of my league,' he whispered to Sophie's bent head.

Jean-Luc's piercing blue eyes flicked from Marco to Sophie, his face a dark mask. Then he nodded coldly in their direction, a brief, indifferent acknowledgement, before guiding his female companion to the waiting car. Sophie watched, her heart numb, as he climbed into the other side of the vehicle. He had not looked again in their direction. Wherever the woman in the evening dress was going at this time of night, Jean-Luc was obviously going too. The car pulled away and vanished down the street. There was nothing left to see.

'Come on, Marco, let's go.' Sophie put her half-eaten burger back in its box and stared at it morosely. Of all the people to stumble into in this big city. And, of course, he was with a gorgeous woman, wearing shoes to die for. Her blonde hair was straightened and moulded with salon precision. Sophie looked down at her own simple white sundress and bare legs and sighed. It was only then that she felt the weight of her friend's arm on her shoulders.

'And why have you got your arm round me?' she asked crossly.

'Nothing personal.' Marco removed his arm, his handsome features unusually hard. 'But that man looks like he needs a lesson. In fact, he looks like a man who's too used to getting it all his own way.'

'Did you see how that woman looked at us? She looked at us like we were trash.'

'Yeah, I saw her staring.' Marco shrugged regally. 'She thinks it's common to eat burgers and fries. That's rich, considering the vulgar way she was draping her cleavage all over that hot boss of yours.'

Sophie said nothing.

'That was your boss, wasn't it?' he continued.

She nodded dully.

'And if I'm not mistaken, your boss is Jean-Luc Olivier?'

Sophie nodded again.

Marco gave a low whistle. 'Sugar, you're in really deep.' He picked up her uneaten burger absent-mindedly and began to finish it off. 'Normally, I don't give people the benefit of my expert advice; but I like you, Sugar, and I want to help you. That guy is in another league, with different rules. Stay away, before you get into trouble.'

'It's too late for that.' Sophie spoke without thinking.

Marco stopped in his tracks. 'Do you mean you've slept with him?'

'No! I mean yes,' she cried. 'Oh, it's not that simple, Marco. It was all a long time ago.'

'That settles it.' Marco threw the empty burger box into a nearby bin. 'We're finding the nearest bar, so you can tell me all about it.'

★ ★ ★

The nearest bar was buzzing, but Sophie hardly noticed. The woman with Jean-Luc had been striking: well-groomed, expensively-dressed, elegant. Everything Sophie was not. The red wine in front of her swirled and clung to the glass as she twisted it absently, explaining the past to her friend. How she'd met Jean-Luc at her eighteenth birthday party. How her rich grandmother had meant well, and genuinely thought that by throwing a party she was doing what was best for Sophie. So, even though she hated being thrust amongst her grandmother's glamorous friends, Sophie had gone through with it to make her grandmother happy, and greeted all her guests with her best smile.

'That is, until he came in,' she said darkly. The wine sloshed over the rim of her glass as she gripped the stem. 'He was just so — so cold. And rude.'

Actually, his rudeness hadn't been overt. His natural courtesy was too innate for that. There was just something there that she couldn't quite put her finger on. The slight curve of his mouth, the merest hint of irony. The dark, tanned face looking down without warmth into hers, his eyes icy blue. Sophie, feeling out of place, her nerves already strung, had met his challenge with a glacial hauteur.

And then when she'd overheard the gossip — that she was her grandmother's poor little Cinderella, on the catch for a rich husband — all vestige of good humour had left her. So that was the cause of his frigid politeness — he thought she was a gold-digger.

Sophie took a gulp from her wine-glass.

'I was furious,' she told Marco. 'What right had he to judge me? He didn't even know me. And why would I want to chase after him, anyway? I don't know anything about racing. I'd never heard of him until that night, and even if I had, I wouldn't have leered all over him like all the other women were doing.'

Sophie's anger hid the full extent of her jangled nerves that evening. In spite of her protestations to Marco, she had found something powerfully attractive about Jean-Luc. And although she kept a wide berth, it seemed the attraction was not just on her side. Whatever she was doing, wherever she was in the room, she knew that if she looked over in his direction his blue eyes would be following her. He stayed in the same place all evening, sitting on a bar stool, surrounded by wave after wave of hangers-on. Unmoving, he watched her. Her nerves prickled unbearably. The music was too loud. She wanted either to escape or to confront him head-on.

'So what happened?'

Sophie looked a little guilty and dropped her eyes to the spots of wine spilt on the table. She dabbed at them ineffectually with a napkin. 'You've got to remember, I was so on edge there was no bearing it anymore. I thought I'd get my own back. Thought I'd teach him a lesson by pretending to be the groupie he thought I was.'

So she confessed to Marco how she'd waited until Jean-Luc got up from his stool and was standing by the edge of the dance floor — alone for once — and seized her moment. And then, when she was just a pace away, how her step faltered a little. He was an imposing man close up. His shoulders were broad, and he carried himself with easy confidence. The fleeting thought had crossed her mind that perhaps her recklessness might get her into trouble.

Then she thought of his scornful assumption about her, and her mouth narrowed into a thin line. With a girlish smile, she'd put her arm round Jean-Luc's waist and looked up at him with what she hoped was a suitably inane expression.

'Not dancing, gorgeous?' She was satisfied to see a startled look cross his proud face and his broad shoulders lean away from her slightly.

'I don't dance, mademoiselle.' His air of cynicism had been replaced by one of caution. Good, Sophie thought viciously. The hunter was about to become the hunted. She snuggled a little closer to him.

'Oh, call me Sophie,' she simpered.

Then suddenly everything changed. He bent his head toward her, one strong arm snaking swiftly around her waist, pulling her to him. Her breath had been knocked out of her in a soft gasp. When she looked up to protest, she found his blue eyes on hers, his expression still unsmiling, his hard features almost frightening in their intensity.

'You're playing a dangerous game, *chérie.*'

From that moment, Sophie was lost.

'I don't know how everything changed,' she told Marco. 'There was something about him . . . It's as though if he decides to do something, somehow it just seems to happen how he wants it — without you realising.' She looked up, her eyes far away. 'And then, when we got outside, he seemed so different somehow. Away from those dreadful groupies and the noise. He was a different man.'

She shivered. Even now, the intensity of that moment could reach forward to her over the years and crush her in its grip. She shut her eyes momentarily. He had turned to lead her across the dance floor, a purposeful progression through the crowds, not stopping until they reached the DJ's booth. Even then, he pulled her forward, behind the booth, until they reached a door set into the far wall. The instant he opened the door and she gazed out into the cool night air, everything else was forgotten. She gasped aloud with pleasure. Like Alice in Wonderland, she stepped outside into a magical country, her white evening dress rustling softly around her long legs. Jean-Luc climbed out after her onto the iron fire-escape, the door shutting behind him with a small clang. The night had been black, but all around them and beneath them and far into the horizon were the lights of Paris, sparkling and turning like jewels caught in a dark glass bowl. The river Seine wound its way through it all, black in the night, unhurried. Above them rose the Eiffel Tower, glittering white and gold. The sounds of the party vanished. The traffic beneath them could barely be heard.

Jean-Luc had smiled at her childish pleasure. The moonlight spilled its silver light over him, softening the harshness of his features. To the teenage Sophie, he was transformed. The cold, arrogant guest had become a devastatingly handsome Prince Charming. He leaned over the balcony railings to point out the various landmarks of Paris for her, his tanned hand outstretched, the sleeve of his jacket brushing against her bare arm. Only when she shivered in the evening breeze had he turned to her. And then he'd taken her in his arms, and her surroundings vanished in the well of her senses. The depth of his kiss engulfed her.

Sophie opened her eyes, willing herself back to the present and the noisy wine bar with a shock. She shivered again. When she dwelt on that evening, an overwhelming sense of longing swept over her. She wished with all her heart she could place herself back in the past, feel the strength of him under her fingers, and hear him whisper her name. That night, at eighteen, she had lived for the moment. The future, in all its drabness, would be oppressing her soon enough. Surely it couldn't be wrong to want a tiny piece of happiness, no matter how fleeting?

So when he came to her hotel room

later that night, she'd let him in, a feverish hunger burning through her, overpowering her shyness. He pulled her to him, more hungrily this time, with a crushing intensity, and a fierceness that was more than matched by her own desire.

Sophie bent her head unhappily.

'What on earth went wrong, Sophie?'

'Marco, can't you see? The next day, I — I knew it was all wrong. He was a young man then, with the whole world at his feet. I was nobody, penniless. I didn't belong there with him. And above all, I had responsibilities. I made my mum a promise to look after my dad and Jack.' She looked up at Marco, her face wretched with unhappiness. 'So, you see, I had to go back. I had no choice.'

Marco sat wide-eyed, his sensitive features mirroring Sophie's unhappiness.

'So what did you do?'

'You don't know how determined he is. He wouldn't let me leave. So in the end, I told him I was engaged.'

Marco looked serious. 'And later he found out you lied. No wonder he came after you.'

Sophie shrugged helplessly. 'I didn't know what else to do. He's a man who's used to everything going his way. It's very hard to stand up to him. He would have made me stay, otherwise, and I would never have forgiven myself.'

She picked up her glass and drained the rest of her wine with a grim look on her face. 'Anyway, that's not all. He thinks I'm an heiress.'

'What?'

'I know.' She looked at Marco hopelessly. 'I thought it would give me a weapon, help me stand up to him, but I've no idea how long I can keep it up.'

'Sugar, you're not going to keep it up. You're going to tell him the truth. Otherwise, that man will chew you up for breakfast and spit out your innocent bones.'

6

Sophie arrived at the mill after the weekend looking pale and drained. But at least she arrived to good news.

Jean-Luc arrived at mid-day to find her sitting with Louisa and Céline on the floor of the designers' office amidst a sea of silk samples and drawings, all three of them chattering away in high animation. His eyes met Sophie's immediately. It was obvious he was in no mood to share whatever it was that excited them. Sophie felt her colour heighten, but Louisa jumped to her feet, blind to the sudden chill in the atmosphere.

'M. Olivier. Guess what? Sophie has organised a visit from Ted Nelson. He's coming next week.'

Ted Nelson was CEO of one of the largest home furnishing suppliers in the States. Their reach was enormous.

Instead of looking suitably impressed, Jean-Luc's face darkened. He moved his gaze back to Sophie. 'What's this about?'

Sophie got slowly to her feet. 'He's in France next week, anyway — ' she began.

Louisa was too excited to let her finish. 'Yes, but Sophie's charmed him into coming here, too. He really wants to meet her.'

Sophie's eyes widened. 'Oh, no, it wasn't that. He's extending his textile collection.'

'So he's coming here,' Jean-Luc said. 'Fine.' He glared at Sophie. 'Next time, copy me in on your emails.'

He turned on his heel and left the room abruptly.

Louisa and Céline stared at each other in astonishment.

'I did copy him in on my emails,' Sophie protested.

'Never mind.' Louisa patted her arm consolingly. 'We always do. He just never reads them.'

Inside his own office, Jean-Luc threw his jacket over the back of his chair and swore. What the hell was the matter with him? The girl had done well. The fact was, he was jealous, pure and simple. He was jealous of the guy he'd seen her with at the weekend. Now he was jealous of Sophie's attentions to Ted Nelson. What a ridiculous emotion. And one he had never in his life experienced. Not with any woman. Ever. They didn't call it the green-eyed monster for nothing — it had him well and truly in its grip.

He swivelled his leather chair round to face the window and stared out, brooding at the hazy sky. It wasn't the fact that the boy she'd been with had had his arm round her that stabbed at him like a knife. It was the fact that they looked so easy in each other's company. How good it would be to be walking along a street with Sophie in that sundress she'd been wearing, just talking, eating French fries. Instead of spending all evening in a suit and tie with a woman welded into thousands of pounds' worth of haute couture.

And the worst thing was, Sophie seemed to be having such genuine fun. For the first time in his life — another first — he hadn't known what to do. Perhaps she wished him miles away? She certainly didn't look happy to see him.

He put his elbows on his knees and his head in his hands. With a great effort of will, he summoned up the resolve to put her from his mind until he had time to deal with it. Just now he had an important visit from the States to think of.

★   ★   ★

Word spread round the mill like wildfire that Sophie had invited an important customer to visit. For the next few days, neither she nor Jean-Luc had any time to dwell on their personal lives. Sophie was struck anew by the passion and commitment he roused in his staff. Within a couple of hours of hearing her news, he had organised the young weavers to come back — on their own time — to give the mill building a clean. Since the workforce apparently included herself, she was instructed with polite firmness to come back in the evening with a change of clothes, and found herself thrown into the frenetic activity along with the rest of the staff. It seemed wherever Sophie looked, Jean-Luc was at the heart of things — solid, in control, calmly commanding the people around him.

Finally, late one evening, she returned to her office after helping with the last touches to the mill building and slumped exhausted into her chair. For a few moments, she closed her weary eyes. What a mess she must look. The cropped top and shorts she was wearing were grimy with dust, and white paint spattered her bare arms and legs. She had tied her hair back roughly in a scarf, but long tendrils were escaping, damp with sweat. She longed for a shower and her bed.

When she heard footsteps approaching, her eyes flew open. Jean-Luc was standing in the doorway. He had joined them that evening in cleaning up the mill and was dressed in a black vest and tattered jeans. His muscles were well-defined under his vest. Like Sophie, he was covered in grime. She shifted her gaze. She'd been trying not to stare at him all evening, and now he had to appear in her small office where she couldn't help but notice how good he looked out of his suit. She made an attempt at flippancy, lifting up her paint-spattered arms for his inspection.

'If I'd known what I was letting myself in for, I'd never have got in touch with Ted Nelson.'

He grinned, his teeth a flash of white. 'And I still haven't thanked you properly. You did really well to persuade him to visit us.'

Jean-Luc didn't give out compliments to his staff unless they were well-deserved. Sophie went pink with pleasure. She was even more surprised when he produced a bottle from behind his back.

'So this is for you, to celebrate your success.'

'Oh wow, champagne.' Her eyes widened at the expensive label.

'Why not?' He smiled indulgently. 'And why so surprised? I thought an heiress like yourself would be drinking champagne all the time.'

'Oh, no, I could never — ' Sophie bit back the words hastily. She had been about to say she couldn't even afford a bottle of cheap white wine at the best of times. She put the bottle down on her table and stood up to face Jean-Luc. She could no longer carry on letting him think she was an heiress. If she were to tell him the truth, it had to be now.

'Jean-Luc, I — '

'It's okay, I know.' He held up one

hand to stop her. For a minute, they both looked at each other in confusion. Sophie felt her cheeks grow warm.

'You know?'

'Look, I saw you in the city with that young man. You don't owe me anything.' He held up his hands. 'I'd just like you to keep our date for the weekend. Come out with me on Saturday.'

Sophie stared at him.

'You've got it all wrong.' She laughed with relief. 'That wasn't what I was going to say. Marco and I aren't dating, we're just friends. And in any case, he's gay.'

Sophie hadn't realised just how tense Jean-Luc must have been. She watched the relief sweep over him, the stiffness disappear from his shoulders, making him look years younger. She could swear his eyes even twinkled.

She lifted her chin. 'Anyway,' she carried on, 'I don't understand what difference it makes. It's not as though you and I are dating. And you see other women.'

Jean-Luc looked puzzled for a moment. 'Do you mean the woman I was with on Saturday?' He raised his eyebrows in astonishment. 'She was a customer — a buyer I took to a business evening.'

'A customer,' Sophie repeated. 'Is that how all customers act when they're around you? In that case, I hope Ted Nelson doesn't drape himself all over you next week.'

'Mademoiselle Challoner, are you jealous?' Jean-Luc bent his head towards her, his mouth lifted in a smile. 'And here I've been torturing myself all week.'

Sophie tilted her chin. 'I'm not jealous. It's none of my business who you go out with.'

'Well, I'd like to go out with you,' he countered, his eyes still dancing. 'So how about coming out with me on Saturday? Have you made up your mind? Do you say yes?'

He stepped closer, and Sophie immediately took a step back. His physical nearness was dangerously persuasive. She needed to keep a clear head.

'What have you got to lose?' he asked, holding his palms up. 'You will get to know me better. And I'd like you to do that, before you judge me.'

Sophie's posture was defensive, but she gave a small, sober nod, her eyes grave. 'Okay, then,' she said. 'I suppose it's only fair.'

Jean-Luc gave a wide, triumphant smile. '*Bon*. Then it's agreed. I'll pick you up at eleven on Saturday.'

In spite of herself, Sophie's dimples reappeared. 'You're incorrigible,' she said. 'I don't even know where we're going.'

'It's a surprise.'

'Well, I need to know what to wear.'

'You women,' he said, rolling his eyes. 'Wear something casual. But more than you have on today, or next time I won't answer for the consequences.' His eyes flicked over her slim body, in her cropped top and shorts, before he turned away sharply.

'Come. Time to go home.'

It wasn't until they left that Jean-Luc remembered Sophie had been about to tell him something. He wondered briefly what it was then shrugged. Certainly, it was nothing. He had already decided she was an innocent.

* * *

Marco's well-groomed head appeared round the door at the sound of Sophie's knock.

'I've got a present for you,' she said, clutching several roll-ends of silk she had salvaged from the weavers' clean-up of the mill. His eyes lit up, then dimmed just as suddenly when he saw the colour.

'Oh, purple,' he grimaced. 'That was two seasons ago.'

'Well, I expect that's why they were getting rid of it at the mill,' Sophie snapped. 'And in any case, beggars can't be choosers.'

'Hey, hey.' He held up his hands. 'What's eating you?'

She dumped the silk on the ground in front of him. 'I've got another date with the boss.' She inserted exaggerated quotation marks with her fingers. 'And he said to wear something casual. I have nothing casual worth wearing. None of the women I've ever seen him with buy their casual clothes at Petticoat Lane market.'

'You'd better come in,' Marco said, understanding immediately the urgency of the situation. He opened his door wide. 'And on second thoughts, bring that silk with you.'

Marco kept his room with an almost obsessive tidiness. Photos of designs he admired were neatly cut out and pinned to his wall and a pile of magazines was stacked by his sewing machine. Sophie stepped forward to inspect one of his drawings.

'That looks like me,' she said in surprise. 'Only much more elegant.'

There was a quick drawing on the

wall of a slim woman wearing a short, midnight-blue dress, her long black hair falling to her waist. The rough sketch was full of beauty.

'It's you exactly as I see you. In fact, you've been a bit of an inspiration.'

'Me?' She turned to face him in amazement. 'Everything I wear is second-hand or bought on the cheap.'

'Sophie, you have style.'

The fashion-obsessed Marco couldn't have given her a greater accolade. Sophie's cheeks turned bright crimson with pleasure.

'But don't go congratulating yourself too soon,' he admonished, his expression becoming serious. He sighed. 'Listen, Sophie, I'm not asking you any questions. And I'm happy to help you all I can. But are you sure you're doing the right thing?'

Sophie looked into her friend's sympathetic eyes, her open features full of uncertainty. 'Oh, I don't know. Maybe you're right — maybe I'm making a big mistake. Don't think I haven't thought about it. Oh, but Marco, I'm only here for a few more weeks. And he makes me feel so alive.'

Marco nodded reluctantly. 'Fine, Sugar. You deserve some fun. I just don't want to see you get hurt, that's all.' He bent down without waiting for her reply and picked up one of the rolls of silk. 'Now, here's what we're going to do,' he continued, throwing the silk outwards in a cascading shimmer of violet. The next minute he was bent over the cloth, scissors in hand, in fierce concentration.

★ ★ ★

It had been agreed (although Sophie was not sure when or how) that instead of skulking outside for her like a criminal, as he expressed it, Jean-Luc would call for her at her room on Saturday morning. When he knocked punctually at eleven, she was ready. He leaned forward in the doorway and kissed her cheek.

171

'You look good.' He did a double-take, holding her at arm's length. 'You look really good. Are you wearing one of my silks?'

'Yes. Is it okay?'

She turned round slowly in front of him. Marco had worked a miracle. The purple silk he had derided had been worked into a shirt-dress, the deep violet an exact match for Sophie's eyes. The supple fabric clung to her curves. She had cinched in her waist with a creamy yellow belt. The whole effect was one of fresh, exotic flowers. She looked radiant.

For a moment, Jean-Luc was speechless. 'Did you make this?' he asked finally.

'No, of course not.' She laughed. 'Marco worked all day on it yesterday. He even went out to buy the buttons specially — look.' She pointed proudly to the large creamy buttons, an exact match to her belt.

'It's a work of art.' Jean-Luc stepped back. 'You look perfect.'

If Jean-Luc was stunned by Sophie's appearance, outside was another surprise: this time for Sophie. She had known Jean-Luc didn't always use his driver. In fact, he preferred to drive himself. She had expected his car to be fast and sporty. Something red, with an open top. Instead, he pointed his remote at the doors of a dull blue family saloon. It wasn't until he'd pulled out into the traffic that he turned his shrewd gaze toward her with a smile.

'You're itching to ask, so why don't you?'

'Ask what?'

'Ask why I'm driving such a boring car.'

Sophie laughed. 'You're right. I didn't think it was quite your style.'

'No, it isn't. When I was younger, I loved fast cars. The racier, the better.'

'And now you've changed?'

'Not at all. I still love fast cars.' He turned his face towards her briefly, his face alight with enthusiasm. Then he sobered, eyes back on the road. 'But I had to give them up. I was attracting dangerous attention. Idiots thinking it was amusing to burn off Jean-Luc Olivier at the lights. When some maniac thought it would be fun to overtake me on a hairpin bend, I knew it was time to lower my profile.'

Sophie digested his words in silence for a few minutes. Very soon after being reunited with Jean-Luc, she had realised he was not the empty thrill-seeker she first thought. On the contrary, he had a steadiness she had never suspected him capable of.

'That's really unfair,' she said. 'If you love cars so much, it's a high price to pay for fame.'

Jean-Luc flicked his gaze her way. 'No one becomes a racing driver for the fame,' he said. 'Quite the opposite. It's a very solitary occupation. Sitting behind the engine, you are totally alone. Your whole focus is on yourself, your car, and winning. After my first few successes, the adulation outside the race track took me a long while to get used to.'

Again Sophie was silenced. She was beginning to realise her teenage visits to her grandmother had tainted her with prejudice. All her assumptions about Jean-Luc's character were being gradually stripped away. He was not the fame-seeker she had thought he was, either. In all his actions, he had shown himself to be an intensely private man.

He broke in on her thoughts now, looking towards her a little hesitantly.

'Sophie, I've been wondering if it's such a good idea to take you with me today.'

Her head twisted round at this. Hesitation was unknown for Jean-Luc. 'What do you mean? Where is it we're going?'

'We're going to a race track. I've been invited to test-drive a new sports car. It's a charity event. The whole point is to raise funds and publicity. There'll be a lot of VIPs there. Cameras, too. If you want to turn back, I'll understand.'

For a couple of seconds, she didn't answer. Then she fished around in her large bag.

'It's okay. I have these.' She brandished a large pair of sunglasses. 'I can hide behind my shades.'

Jean-Luc acknowledged her bright response, but without returning her smile. A troubled expression crossed his face briefly, before he turned his attention to the road ahead.

Sophie took advantage of his preoccupation to run through a mental list of the clothes she was wearing. A sudden attack of nerves assailed her. Her exposure to her grandmother's circle had made her hypersensitive to any reflection on the cheapness of her clothes. She knew it was superficial, and she ought to rise above it, but inside she was grateful to Marco for her silk dress. Her cream handbag was fine, too — vintage 1950s and one of her grandmother's. That just left her shoes — flat pumps bought off Camden Market. She'd just come to the decision that the rest of her outfit meant she could probably risk the cheap shoes, when Jean-Luc broke in on her thoughts.

'What are you mulling over there so quietly?'

She turned her head. There was only a slight hesitation before she spoke. 'I was just thinking what a brilliant job Marco did with my dress.'

At least there was an element of truth in that. The rest of her worries she kept to herself.

She had made a half-cowardly bargain with herself — she would enjoy whatever the day with Jean-Luc had to offer and only at the end of it confess that she wasn't the heiress he thought. She just hoped by then he would understand.

Jean-Luc swept his gaze appraisingly down the violet dress clinging to her slim frame. 'That young man will go far. I'd like to meet him some time.'

Sophie raised her eyes to Jean-Luc's profile, glad of an excuse to change the subject. Her expression full of mischief, she made her reply as offhand as possible.

'Oh, I'm not sure he'd be interested. Actually, he thinks you're not good enough for me.'

'What?' He turned towards her for a full couple of seconds, and Sophie was amused to see that, for once, he was thunderstruck.

'Don't you think you'd better keep your eyes on the road?' she asked innocently.

His head twisted back, his hands gripping the wheel. 'What a salutary experience it is, being in your company. Until I met you, I had no idea I was such a lowlife.'

Sophie registered the asperity in his reply and felt a twinge of guilt. 'Marco's a good friend,' she said. 'He just doesn't want to see me hurt.'

'And, of course, I'm the sort of person who'd deliberately go out of his way to hurt you?'

She hesitated before answering. She

was quite sure he was not the type of man to hurt anyone. Not deliberately. But he swept people before him, men and women, on the tide of his own will. He was the sort of man it was dangerous to be caught up with.

Jean-Luc glanced down at her. 'Sophie, I know the stories the newspapers print. If I'm seen out with another woman, it makes a good photo. And I have dated other women.'

He noticed the faint frown on her face. 'Well, for heaven's sake!' he expostulated. 'That doesn't make me a monster. There must have been other men in your life, too.'

There was a short silence before Sophie raised her clear features. There was something about the intimacy of travelling with him this way, in the closed car, that made her feel safe. Safe enough to confess what she had never told anyone.

'There haven't been any other men,' she said simply. 'Apart from you.'

His eyes widened, and there was an

infinitesimal lurch in the direction of the car. His head flicked her way for an instant, and then his eyes were back on the road. She waited for him to speak. When he said nothing, she spoke herself. 'Do you think it strange?'

'No, *chérie*,' he said gently. He turned his dark head toward her. 'It's your choice. And I think it's an incredibly touching choice. But you're a beautiful woman. Other men must have wanted you.'

Beautiful. Sophie's clear violet eyes were fixed on the windscreen, watching the autoroute ahead race past them. No one had ever made her feel that way before. And never a man like Jean-Luc, who had known many beautiful women. She stored the compliment carefully with her other memories.

'After my mother died, I was always too busy for a relationship,' she explained. 'And I grew up too quickly. Men my age seemed much too young.'

She didn't reveal the full truth.

What would he think if she confessed she'd been clinging to a wild teenage dream? That the night he kissed her in the moonlight had been replayed in her head over and over again, and that he'd played the role of Prince Charming, which no other man could live up to? She stole a look at his profile and, for the first time, began to wonder if her own extravagant dream could really come true. Then she shrugged and turned away, hiding the hardening of her features. He always made her feel like this — like there was no barrier between them. In a few weeks' time, she would be back in London, facing her own reality. A reality that had no room for fairytales.

The gentleness was still present in Jean-Luc's voice as he answered her.

'You're still young, too, Sophie. Perhaps it's good you came here to France. You can escape your troubles for a little while.'

'It's not that easy.' She thought of

Jack's increasingly worrying phone calls.

Jean-Luc nodded. 'I know what it is to give up your youth,' he said. There was an infinitesimal hesitation before he continued. 'My mother was ill for many years before she died.'

'I'm sorry you lost her,' Sophie said. She sensed there was something more, something Jean-Luc was reluctant to add, and wondered how much he was willing to talk about his own personal tragedy. She made her response studiedly noncommittal. 'I hope it wasn't a painful illness.'

Jean-Luc thought of the bloated, yellowing figure in the hospital bed, the years he'd spent trying to protect his mother before she finally self-destructed, and he felt again the terror he had felt at that time, watching impotently as the person he loved slipped out of his control. He took in a sharp breath.

'I tried to protect her from herself.' His voice was suddenly harsh. 'But nothing I did was any use.'

Sophie turned round, horrified eyes on him. He glanced over. When he caught sight of her expression, he forced his dark features to relax.

'I'm sorry. We shouldn't be talking of such things.' He smiled. 'I want you to enjoy the day.'

For the rest of the journey, he resolutely kept the conversation light. They talked about films they had seen, parts of France they had visited, sightseeing in London. The brief insight Sophie had gained into his troubled past might never have happened. If she had wanted to touch on the tragedy of his youth, he would have batted the subject away; but in any case, it was obvious Sophie had anxieties of her own during the journey which she was evidently trying to subdue.

As they approached the race track, Jean-Luc realised she was becoming increasingly quiet. She had picked up on the attention they were receiving from other drivers — some content with no more than an excited glance in Jean-Luc's direction, others dropping behind or slowing in front of them to stare outright. As Jean-Luc pulled up outside the glass-fronted building and cut the engine, he turned to her.

'Are you okay?'

She nodded, her face a little pale. 'There are a lot of people here, aren't there?'

He lifted her chin, holding it lightly in his warm hand. 'I'm here with you, don't forget.' He smiled encouragingly. 'There's nothing to worry about. You'll knock them dead.'

* * *

The next half an hour passed in a blur for Sophie. Once inside the hospitality suite, she was introduced to several men in suits, and a glass of champagne was pressed into her hand. She sipped at it gratefully, hoping it would steady her nerves. There was a buffet laid out on the table for them and someone handed her a plate filled with food. She barely touched it.

Wherever Jean-Luc went, a buzz followed. Among the men in suits were several mechanics who pressed round him, shaking his hand and talking with animation. Sophie was just beginning to relax — there was nothing threatening here, no one was even taking any notice of her — when she found herself being ushered outside with the others. They emerged in the middle of one of the stands, which was full of spectators. As soon as they appeared, a hundred cameras whirred into action.

Jean-Luc took her arm to guide her down the concrete stairway. In front of them, in the middle of the track, was a white sports car. Sophie made to stop when they reached the bottom of the stairs, to join the others in the crowd, but Jean-Luc propelled her forward.

'Come.' He smiled. His eyes were brilliant in the sunshine. She felt the controlled excitement underneath his composure and, for a moment, forgot the onlookers enough to smile up at him. The cameras carried on whirring.

Jean-Luc led her across the track. Even to Sophie's inexpert eye, the car was something else. Its curvaceous shell flowed from front to rear, finishing with an unusual engine, which gleamed under glass, inches away from the driver's seat. Jean-Luc walked over to inspect it, the mechanics and men in suits eager to show off the engine's finer points. Once again, Sophie was about to turn back when she saw Jean-Luc say something to a mechanic, and beckon her over. The men fell back slightly. Jean-Luc opened the passenger door.

'Get in.' He gestured toward the car.

Sophie's mouth fell open. Before she could say anything, he had his arm round her and was guiding her to the passenger seat which, to Sophie's mind, was perilously close to the ground.

'Are you sure this is safe?' she whispered furiously.

He laughed. 'Trust me.'

She dropped down into the low-slung

leather seat and felt Jean-Luc take his place beside her. There was no time to register what was happening. Excitement was flowing from Jean-Luc in palpable waves. The engine started with a roar just behind her head. She gasped.

'Ready?'

Before she could answer, his foot was on the pedal, and Sophie felt her whole body shoot back with something close to G-force. In an instant, the stands disappeared, and they were out on the open track, the black tarmac racing by dangerously close to eye level. Jean-Luc accelerated, and the engine's roar increased to a thunder reverberating around her ears. The advertising hoardings whipped by overhead with incredible speed. When they cornered the first bend, Sophie almost screamed aloud with exhilaration and fear. Her hands clutching the creamy leather seat beside her bare knees, she turned to look at Jean-Luc. He was staring at the road ahead in intense concentration, completely absorbed. She felt the all-consuming thrill of being swept along by him course through her and the powerful, heady, breathtaking release of giving herself up completely to his control. She leaned back in her seat and surrendered utterly to the sensation of speed, her long hair whipping around her head, her breath almost sucked out of her body.

Before she knew it, the stands were approaching rapidly, the engine's roar was dying, and Jean-Luc was easing the car gently back into the exact spot from which they'd started. For the couple of minutes they shared alone, before the racing mechanics reached the car, they stared at each other.

'That was . . . was . . . ' She gave up on words. Her smile split her face.

Jean-Luc grinned back. The next minute, the car was surrounded, her door was opening, and one of the mechanics was helping her out on her shaky legs.

'Sophie.' Jean-Luc called her back. 'Wait in the stands for me. I'm going to put the car through its paces.'

'Haven't we done that already?' Sophie asked.

One of the mechanics laughed as the car door closed. 'That was a Sunday drive, mademoiselle. This car can do real speed.'

She retreated, and the sports car shot off into the distance. When the noise of the engine's roar had disappeared, Sophie climbed back up the concrete steps to stand with a group of spectators. She was so wrapped up in watching out for the return of Jean-Luc that it was some time before she realised it was she, and not the car's driver, who was the object of attention in the glamorous group surrounding her. There was some not-so-quiet whispering, and then one of the women approached her, effortlessly elegant in her high heels.

'So, you must be Jean-Luc's new *petite amie*.' A pair of hard green eyes, with heavy mascara, swept over her with breathtaking coldness. Sophie registered one of the other women in the group sniggering behind a manicured hand. She lifted her chin.

'I'm a friend of Jean-Luc's, yes.'

'Oh we've all been Jean-Luc's friend at some time or other, darling.' The words were slightly slurred, and Sophie wondered how many glasses of champagne the young woman had drunk. 'But you're not his usual style.' She stared down at Sophie's cheap pumps in disdain. 'He must be scraping the barrel now that he's retired.'

Sophie schooled her expression behind her sunglasses. Courageous and determined under any other circumstances — she had just been driven round a race track at close to two hundred miles an hour, and had revelled in the experience — at this moment she felt as she always did when made the butt of vicious bitchiness: physically sick. Her hands began to tremble, and she stared into the cold, hard eyes confronting her, unable to think of a single retort.

Feeling the blood drain from her face, she turned her back on the woman's sneer and began to make her way back up the stairs to the hospitality room. A camera's shutter whirred in her face and she heard a man's voice cry out insistently. She took no notice.

The hospitality box was empty when she re-entered it. She helped herself to a glass of water with shaking hands and went to the window, to watch for Jean-Luc.

7

It wasn't long before Jean-Luc was back — three or four laps, which he completed at breathtaking speed — but still it seemed the event wasn't over. A small podium had been erected, in front of which a couple of the men in suits were waiting with a large cheque. Jean-Luc spoke briefly in front of a banner supporting his charity. Sophie noted with dull surprise it was for recovering addicts. Jean-Luc had so much iron control himself, it was difficult to imagine him sympathising with those unfortunate people who had lost control of their lives to drink or drugs; but by now, Sophie was inured to the fact that she was constantly underestimating him.

There was a ripple of applause and more handshakes, and then he was mounting the concrete steps. Even then, Sophie's wait continued. A swarm of people, some clutching autograph books, was eager to meet him. With dismay, she saw the two women who'd accosted her elbowing their way toward him with frightening determination. She watched Jean-Luc greet them with one of his small, charming smiles. One of the women wriggled her arms around his neck and planted a passionate kiss on his lips. It was obvious Jean-Luc knew them both. And from the woman's body language, he knew them very well indeed.

He disentangled himself, holding the woman at arm's length, but with a friendly enough smile on his face. Sophie watched as he scanned the crowds above the blonde woman's head, then lifted his eyes towards the hospitality box. The next minute he had abandoned the women and was running lightly up the steps. A faint frown was on his face as he entered, quickly replaced by a look of concern.

'Why are you hiding in here?' he asked.

Sophie's face was pale, but she met him with a smile. 'It was just a little hot out there.'

Jean-Luc cast a quick glance outside, to where the stand was actually in full shade, but made no comment. By now, he recognized Sophie's brave face when he saw it.

'Want to go home?' Her grateful smile was all the reply he needed. 'Come, let's make our escape.'

Back on the autoroute, when Jean-Luc asked her if she'd enjoyed her drive, she turned to him, eyes shining, but her happy response was short-lived. It wasn't long before she was staring out of the window again. Although from time to time she made bright, sporadic comments about the scenery they passed or the music on the radio, Jean-Luc sensed she had retreated into her shell. After half an hour, he left the road, jolting Sophie out of her abstraction.

'Where are we going?'

'Just taking a detour.' He kept his words light, so as not to alarm her, and spun the car off the slip road and down onto a country track.

The sun had fallen low in the sky and long shadows reached out over the heat-dried fields. A barrier of woodland passed between Sophie and the worst of the sun's dying rays, and bright light flickered through the green of the trees. Jean-Luc pulled into a shady lay-by, wound down the windows, and cut the engine. Warm air and the smell of long grass flooded the car. The hum of the autoroute could be heard in the distance.

Sophie turned to him, eyes wide with enquiry. 'What is it?' He unfastened his seat belt and turned his upper body toward her. The sinking sun cast golden flecks over Sophie's hair as she shifted in her seat.

'I don't know,' he said. 'You tell me.'

Jean-Luc spoke quietly, but he had that unyielding expression Sophie was beginning to recognise. She drew in her breath, but he cut her off, threading his fingers through the hair at the nape of her neck and turning her head so her eyes met his.

'Come, Sophie. Something's been troubling you. Was I right about the cameras? Was that it?'

'No. No, it wasn't that.' She felt his probing gaze on hers, the warmth of his hand insistent on the nape of her neck.

'Okay,' she relented. 'It wasn't the cameras. It's the rest of it. It's all the people who surround you. It's not my world, Jean-Luc. I don't belong in it.'

She watched him draw back, registered his surprise, and then she stumbled on, desperate to finish before a treacherous tremor appeared in her voice.

'When I was a teenager, visiting my grandmother, her house was full of friends just like the women who were at the race track today. She called them friends, but really they were just with her because she had money. And to them, I was a common little nobody who cramped my grandmother's designer style.'

Sophie stopped. It was impossible to carry on. How to explain to a man of Jean-Luc's masculine self-confidence the torture she had felt as a self-conscious teenage girl? About the sneers she had endured just because of a cheap handbag? Or for wearing low-price jeans? At an impressionable age, her grandmother's friends had made her feel cheap. By the time she was old enough to understand how superficial it all was, it was too late. The damage had been done. Sophie had acquired an aloof exterior which hid a deep sensitivity to snide remarks and bitching.

Jean-Luc's nostrils flared with anger. 'I know exactly what those bitches at the race track can be like, believe me. But what was your grandmother think-ing of, to expose you like that?'

Sophie shook her head. 'I know my grandmother was vain and silly, but she had no real friends. In her own way, she needed me.' She added fiercely, 'And I promised my mum I would take care of the family, and that included her mother.'

Jean-Luc sat back in his seat, his expression grim. 'So what happened this afternoon?'

'Oh, nothing much. Just some women making comments. They told me they'd been friends of yours. You certainly seemed to know one of them very well.'

Jean-Luc cursed. He turned to Sophie and took both her hands in his strong grip.

'It's true I dated one of those women for a time. But it was a long time ago, and it meant nothing. We both knew the score. I took her out, and she enjoyed spending my money.'

Sophie was side-tracked. 'You mean you bought her?' She tried to keep the incredulity from her voice.

Jean-Luc's colour heightened under his tan. 'That wasn't ... Good grief — ' He broke off, discomfited.

'What an extraordinary girl you are. Listen, I was younger than you are now when I suddenly acquired money and fame. So what if that attracted beautiful women? I wasn't going to turn them away. I don't know many young men that would.'

'So,' Sophie said slowly, her mind turning over this new piece of information, 'how do you know whether a woman's going out with you because she likes you, or because she likes your money and fame?'

'What a terrible picture you have of me.' He laughed, a harsh, self-deprecating sound. 'Well, it's true. I had a lot of girlfriends. I enjoyed them and they enjoyed spending my money. It was a simple equation.'

Sophie looked aghast. 'That sounds . . .' She struggled to put it into words. 'That sounds so ordered. So controlled.'

Jean-Luc considered her words and relented slightly. 'Perhaps you're right,' he said. 'Maybe I was a rather cold young man in those days. But now it's different.' He reached a hand up to her cheek. 'You do me good, *chérie*. You always speak the truth.'

His words caused the blood to drain from Sophie's face. She thought of the lie she had told him and twisted free from his grasp, but he caught her, holding her head in his hands so that she was forced to look at him.

'I haven't been honest!' she blurted out. 'I wasn't upset because you've slept with one of those women. Well,' she continued truthfully, 'I was a bit upset. But I know you've had other girl-friends.'

'Then what was it?'

Sophie gave him a look that was half-hesitant, half-defiant. 'If I tell you, promise you'll try and understand.'

'I'll try,' he said.

'It's because they were laughing at my shoes.'

'Your shoes?' He dropped his hands to his sides and gave a laugh of amazement.

'I know,' she cried. 'I know it's silly

200

and vain and shallow to get upset about shoes. But I can't afford to dress like those women can. And I'm absolutely sick to death of thinking about money!'

Jean-Luc watched with horror as her eyes flooded with tears. 'Why were they laughing at your shoes? You look gorgeous,' he said. 'And what do you mean you can't afford to? I don't understand. You told me your grandmother made you her heiress.'

'Well she didn't. I lied.' Her shoulders began shaking.

'But why on earth would you lie?' His blue eyes were wide and searching. 'I don't understand. Why?'

'Because you goaded me into it! You said I was a gold-digger. And at that party everyone thought I was a poor nobody getting married for money, and I'm sick of people thinking that about me because it's not true.'

Now her misery was unmistakable. Great gulping sobs racked her. She buried her face in her hands. 'It's always about money in your world.' She was crying so much now he could barely distinguish her words. 'That's why I don't belong here.'

'Sophie, Sophie. Surely you know money doesn't matter to me. Why did you lie to me? I don't care.'

'It's alright for you to say money doesn't matter,' she sobbed wildly. 'It doesn't matter if you've got it. But if you haven't, in your world, everyone looks at you like you're nothing.'

'Sophie,' he said huskily. He caught hold of her hands and, in spite of her resistance, bore them down from her face. 'You're not nothing.'

He moved the ball of his thumb gently over her tears and down to her mouth, to still the sobs that escaped her. His fingers caressed her wet cheeks slowly until the painful sobs had ceased, and she felt herself swaying towards him, the liquid warmth of his touch stealing into her body and flooding through her. He caught hold of her face as she moved and tilted it upward to meet his.

'This is all that matters.'

And then he was bending his head towards her, and his warm lips were on hers in a kiss. The strength of his hands on her face held such certainty, a conviction echoed in the depth of his kiss, the determination in his eyes as he'd lowered his face to hers, drawing her to him. She felt herself responding to his strength, pressing her lips to his for his kiss, and a groan escaped from him. His arms tightened around her, engulfing her, and her mouth parted at last under his.

She held him, her face still wet with her tears, and felt his warm hands exploring her body, sliding down to her waist. He pulled her closer, holding her tight to his hard body as though somehow she might escape his arms.

A car approached, bumping up the country track. Jean-Luc broke away with a ragged gasp before pulling Sophie back into his arms and pressing her face to his chest. He turned his upper body so their faces were both shielded from view.

'Stay still.'

Sophie's face was muffled in his shirt. She heard his heart thudding under her cheek and smelt the warm, musky smell of him, his arms wrapped around her. After a time, he moved her gently out of his embrace, smoothing her long hair where it had become entangled in his arms.

'Are you okay?' he asked quietly.

She nodded. He watched the car disappearing up the road ahead of them.

'I think we've had enough cameras for today,' he said.

Sophie stared at him. 'Did they have a camera?'

He moved back into his own seat, reaching for his belt.

'I don't know.' He shrugged and turned to look at her. 'Everyone has a camera these days.'

Suddenly, he seemed remote. The intimacy between them had been shattered. Sophie turned away. Her heart had still not slowed its rapid beating, and her senses were painfully on edge. Without Jean-Luc's arms around her, she felt cold. Her fingers trembled slightly as she clicked her belt into place. She stole a look at Jean-Luc's profile. He was manoeuvring the car with precision in the narrow road, one arm flung over the back of her chair to reverse, his expression unsmiling and almost grim.

Sophie felt the familiar constriction of unhappiness in her chest and the tears prickled again behind her eyelids. It had been Jean-Luc's intention for her to get to know him better today, but she already knew all about his world. And she knew, with painful clarity, that it was not a world where she could ever feel at home. Their day together had simply confirmed it.

She turned her face away to stare out at the darkening fields. A few minutes later, they were back on the autoroute. Sophie gripped her hands together in her lap until the knuckles showed white.

How cowardly and insecure she must seem to him. He had thought she would enjoy herself, have a few glasses of champagne with the other girls and relax with the crowd. Instead, he had found her hiding away by herself, waiting pathetically until he got back. She thought of the many other girls he had dated and the gossip-mag photos of his confident women, smiling and relaxed with the cameras, and inside, she winced. She had come to anticipate comments about her background with an almost phobic dread.

As a teenager, she had learned not to speak of it to her family and to pretend it was not important. Her father was ill, and he could not have borne to hear of Sophie's pain on top of his own depression. Her brother was too young, and they had only just lost their mother. And so she had put a brave face on things, internalising the experience of rejection, only to find it

206

resurfacing with increasing regularity, bound up with the loss of her mother and her father's withdrawal.

She stole another look at Jean-Luc, his eyes on the road ahead, his mouth set, and imagined what it would be like if he rejected her as well. Her face whitened. She wondered what on earth had possessed her to go so far down this road with him. Again, the feeling of being swept helplessly along on the tide of his volition came over her. Then she shook herself. Deep down, she had no one to blame but herself. Even her friend Marco had warned her to stay away.

She turned back to the window. They were on the outskirts of Lyon, and soon they would be back at her student residence. Ever since the car had passed them in the lay-by, Jean-Luc had become increasingly withdrawn. Sophie felt a lurch of pain, followed by the familiar sensation of her exterior shell creeping over the wound. She lifted her chin. So now he knew what she'd known all along: they came from different worlds. They would both just have to forget it. Move on.

She clamped her uplifted chin tightly shut on the rising tears.

Jean-Luc guided the car expertly into a parking space outside her hall and jumped out without speaking. She had barely undone her seatbelt when he appeared at the passenger door, holding it wide for her. He extended one strong, brown hand to help her out. Once on the pavement, he lifted his hands to her upper arms to hold her lightly.

'You're tired, *chérie*.' He stroked his fingers lightly over her cheek.

'Thanks for the drive,' Sophie said. 'It was awesome.' For a brief instant, her dimples reappeared, along with the former light in her eyes. Then it dimmed just as suddenly. She felt all the awkwardness of the situation. To say the day had not gone well was an understatement.

Jean-Luc stepped forward.

'Good night, Sophie.' He pulled her

forward and kissed her lips softly. Sophie felt his arms hold her in a brief, close embrace. 'Don't worry, *chérie*. There's nothing so bad I can't fix it.'

Sophie unlocked her doors and watched him return to his car through the glass. As she replaced her keys in her bag, she noticed a missed call on her mobile. Jack again. Head bent with weariness, she mounted the stairs to her room. In spite of Jean-Luc's reassurance, her heart was cold and heavy with foreboding, and she doubted even he, with all his determination, could lighten it.

★ ★ ★

By the time Jean-Luc had crossed the city's two rivers to reach his own apartment, dusk had settled firmly over the old town. His flat was in shadow, but he didn't illuminate it. Instead, he threw his jacket over the back of his leather chair, poured himself a cognac, and took it over to the wide bay windows, where a gathering gloom fell on the river beneath. Red and orange lights glittered in the lanes of traffic below him, and a heavily-laden barge was making its way up the black river. Jean-Luc stared out over the city, mouth set in a grim line.

Of all the idiotic things to do. He should have known Sophie would feel ill-at-ease in such an environment. Wear something casual, he'd said. He should have stressed *something that won't attract the photo lenses*. He'd never expected her to come out of her room looking like a million dollars.

He gazed down at the amber liquid in his glass, his irritation with himself growing. Whatever she wore, it would have made no difference. She'd looked stunning in the grubby shorts she'd worn to clean the mill.

And then when he thought back to the night he'd met Sophie, to the glittering recklessness in the teenage girl, he cursed himself for not recognising her façade for what it was.

And now, to cap his folly, this afternoon he had kissed her. He drew in his breath. In spite of her reserve, he knew how responsive she would be to his touch. Her soft body had yielded under his when he kissed her, and he had known how easy it would be to break down her barriers and take her.

For the whole day, he had been intensely aware of every inch of her. The smooth movement of her long legs when she crossed them, the silk clinging to her thighs, the elegant line of her neck when she turned away from him. The way the neckline of her dress opened slightly when she moved . . .

Now, in the shadows of his room, his mind was filled with the darkest fantasies of bending her yielding body to his will, of not letting her leave until she gave herself to him body and soul. There would be no running away if he kept her here. Then his lips twisted, and he lifted his cognac. Good God, with his mind brooding on thoughts like these it was no wonder she shied away from him. He drained his glass in one fell swoop and threw himself into his armchair, his long legs sprawling in front of him.

When she'd confessed he'd been her only lover, he felt such a surge of fierce protectiveness, he'd been almost undone. He grimaced at the irony. The one person she needed protecting from was himself. He twisted his empty cognac glass round and round in his long fingers. It was clear to him that if he wanted to keep her, to stop her running away from him again, he must find some way of protecting her from his environment. The people who surrounded him at the race track were not his friends, but they were a part of his fame, something Sophie would inevitably have to face. And he knew now for certain that he wanted Sophie in his life. The thought he might be in love entered his mind and was swiftly banished. Love was not an emotion that he could make fit in his neatly-controlled world.

He leaned back in his chair, resting his head, his eyes on some point in the distance. To an outside observer he would have appeared still, relaxed even, but his quick mind was revolving and planning in a way that would have exasperated Sophie if she were present.

Jean-Luc's upbringing had had its own tragedies, but lack of money wasn't one of them. He would happily buy Sophie dozens of pairs of shoes — a whole shoe shop full of them — if he thought it would make her happy. He could give her as much money as she wanted, but he knew instinctively that this was not the answer. Making her feel indebted to him was not the way to win her.

For a long while he sat, immobile, in the gathering darkness. Then he sat up straight, his hard features relaxing with a warmth that filled his eyes with a steely glow. He had hit on a solution which would have had Sophie, had she known about it, utterly dumbfounded.

* * *

Blissfully unaware her life was being mapped out for her again by Jean-Luc, Sophie arrived for work early, tired and subdued but looking neat as a new pin in her suit. Today was the day their important contact in the U.S. was due to visit the mill.

She had spent Sunday trying to prepare for the visit and had come to the conclusion that when she eventually left Lyon and Jean-Luc behind, she should resign herself to never having any sort of relationship. If this was what dating was all about, then it was totally incompatible with a career. Her ability to concentrate was zero, and Marco was no help at all. Ever since she'd told him how much Jean-Luc had admired her dress, he had veered wildly between a vigorous defence of Jean-Luc's excellent judgment on all things and *I told you so*, with no sensible middle ground in between.

A late-night phone call from Jack had capped off a dreadful weekend. He had called out the doctor to their father, who had slumped back into a depression and was not eating. The situation had improved over the past few days with their father's new medication, but Sophie agreed with a reluctant Jack that if it worsened again, she should return to London. Her brother was practising hard for his music competition and, in the circumstances, was coping really well. Their father's depression was something they'd both lived with for years, but something about the present situation, some deep-rooted instinct, had Sophie more concerned than usual.

She was staring out of the window when she heard Jean-Luc enter her office. Something in her abstraction must have alerted him, because he stepped forward quickly.

'Everything okay?'

She turned, rearranging her features

into an automatic smile, and he held up one hand.

'The truth, Sophie.'

She had the grace to look a little sheepish. 'Sorry, automatic reaction. I'm not used to sharing my worries.'

'I told you before, I have very broad shoulders.'

'I know.' She hesitated. Omitting the fact that her worries included Jean-Luc himself, she submitted part of the truth. 'It's my dad. He's not well again. I'm wondering whether I should go home.'

'Go home?' Jean-Luc started forward. 'I understand you must be worried. But surely your brother . . . ?'

'Yes, of course there's Jack. But he's got an important music competition coming up. And in any case . . . ' She shrugged, resigned. 'Well, now isn't the time for worrying. We've got our visitor.'

'Sophie.' Jean-Luc's brows drew together. 'If you need to go home, you must go. But I don't want to lose you.'

Something in the way he said the words had Sophie's eyes flying to his face. Was he saying that as an employer? Or something else? Before she could reply, Céline's auburn head appeared round the door. She stared curiously from Jean-Luc to Sophie before announcing: 'M. Olivier, our visitor is in reception.'

The rest of the day flew by.

Their visitor, Ted Nelson, turned out to be a charming elderly gentleman with an old-world courtesy, determined to be pleased with everything he saw. His gentle manner hid an astute mind, and Sophie was kept busy translating his soft, southern drawl into the rapid French spoken by all around her. By the end of the day she was stumbling occasionally, her words tumbling over each other, and she felt Jean-Luc's watchful eyes on her. But she recovered lightly enough, and Mr Nelson had seen enough to find her hesitation charming.

When he finally left to catch his plane

back to the States, with more than the promise of placing a large order, the day was proclaimed a sound success. After congratulating Irina and the weavers for their contribution, Jean-Luc opened a bottle of champagne in the designers' office and proposed a toast. 'To Pascha Silks.'

The designers chorused their approval. After a day spent talking, the champagne felt cool and crisp in Sophie's throat. She gave an unconscious sigh of pleasure. Jean-Luc's blue eyes gleamed over the rim of his glass.

'And now, to the girl who charmed our important visitor. To Sophie,' he said softly.

Céline and Louisa exchanged knowing smiles before raising their glasses again. 'To Sophie.'

Sophie dimpled with pleasure. She smiled at Jean-Luc, raising her glass to his, determined to enjoy the moment. Whatever the future might bring for her, at least she could share his present happiness in their success. She had been storing up moments such as these, a sort of memory deposit bank, so that when she was back at home in London she would have a secret stash of treasures to pore over.

For the next few days, Jean-Luc was again away on business, this time in Italy. Sophie's days were occupied enough without him, but she couldn't help noticing how empty the mill was without his presence. She caught herself looking at her calendar, counting the days until he reappeared, and then shook herself. Her placement was rapidly nearing its close, and there would be time enough to miss him when she was back in London. She would have to get used to the idea of a life without Jean-Luc.

And just when she had thought she had enough problems to mull over, there was more to come. She arrived home one evening to hear Marco calling out to her from across the corridor.

'Sugar, come and look at this!'

He was brandishing a magazine, in a

state of high excitement, and had obviously been waiting on tenterhooks for her return. He thrust the magazine into her hands. 'Take a look.'

It was one of France's weekly gossip mags. Sophie scanned the headlines. A film star was about to divorce; one of France's biggest pop stars welcomed readers into her stylish home; a game show host was expecting a baby. They were the usual stories. Sophie looked up, puzzled. There was nothing here to get excited about.

'Read on.' He pointed to the call-out under the cover shot.

The Return of Violet. The text was written in bold under a photo of an English model. The dark-haired girl was wearing a cotton shirt, similar in colour to the dress Sophie had worn to the race track. She looked beautifully chic.

'Oh, I see. So purple's back in fashion, after all.' Sophie smiled, pleased for Marco. 'Cool.' She proffered him the magazine, but he thrust it into her hands.

'No, that's not all. Have a look at the spread.' He ripped the magazine from her hands impatiently, and opened it under her nose. 'Here.'

Chic in Violet ran the title, underneath which were photos of various models and celebrities all wearing purple, and . . . oh. There, under Marco's outstretched finger, was a photo of herself and Jean-Luc in the sports car. It was obviously taken at the end of their ride. She was turning to Jean-Luc with a wide, triumphant smile. His back was angled to the camera, and he was looking down at her, his wide shoulders filling out the white shirt he was wearing.

Sophie felt a slow, deep flush of mortification mount as she stared at the photo. To an outside observer, it appeared as though she were looking up at Jean-Luc with nothing less than adoration. Their brief moment, which Sophie had thought private, had been snapped and sold and published. Her feelings were displayed nakedly, for all to see. What if Jean-Luc himself happened to buy the magazine? She closed her eyes briefly, the mortification rippling through her. If she had been worrying that Jean-Luc thought her unsophisticated, her girlish expression of hero-worship in this photo was the final nail in her coffin.

There was worse to come.

Her eyes fell on the brief article beneath the photo.

Who's that girl causing such a stir at the race track? Our friends inform us she's Sophie Challoner, granddaughter of socialite Monique Limantour, who passed away recently. Parisians will remember Mme Limantour's determined efforts to introduce her granddaughter to Europe's most eligible bachelors. We are happy to see Sophie has landed her man at last — congratulations Sophie!

There followed a footnote: *Jean-Luc's former girlfriend, Natasha Volkova, was unavailable for comment.* It was accompanied by a photo of a beautiful Russian model staring wistfully into the distance, her high cheekbones and deep blue eyes giving all the appearance of someone whose heart had been tragically broken.

Sophie read the article again in disbelief. Without saying as much in words, they had made Sophie out to be a social climber who had trodden ruthlessly over Jean-Luc's previous girlfriend in order to get her clutches on him. The vicious rumours she had thought forgotten were alive and had resurfaced. Sophie closed her eyes, her slim hands gripping the magazine.

8

'Sophie, are you alright?'

Marco's words brought her to her senses. She opened her eyes, blinking back the tears.

'No, of course not, Marco. How could you think I would be? What they've said is horrible.'

'Oh, that.' Marco looked at her, a little sheepish. He attempted belatedly to console her. 'It's nothing to worry about,' he said. 'No one who knows you would ever believe you're like that.'

His words sounded a little empty, and they both knew it. Sophie stared at him white-faced for a moment, then jumped as a thought flashed through her.

'Jean-Luc!' Her face flushed crimson at the thought of what he might think if he read the article. 'And Dad and Jack.

I'd better phone them before they find out.'

She ran into her room, throwing the offending magazine onto her bed in her haste to get to her phone. When she finally spoke to Jack, he was typically sanguine. If Sophie were honest, he was a little too sanguine. She desperately needed advice and sympathy, but knew she was being unreasonable. A few bitchy words in a French magazine held none of the pain for Jack that they did for Sophie. He was already worried enough about their dad's illness and his coming competition. Halfway through their conversation, Sophie decided, as usual, that it was best to suppress her own needs beneath her habitual cheerful banter. Even so, when Jack finished off their talk with his usual cheery exhortation to her to stay out of trouble, she nearly burst into tears.

She had had enough of coping. She put the phone down and, catching sight of the offending magazine lying open at her smiling picture, picked it up off her bed and hurled it at the wall. Then she threw herself face-down on the pillow. If ever she needed her mother back, now was the time. She squeezed her eyes shut against the hot tears that were rolling down her cheeks. It was time she recognised the truth: she was in love, desperately in love, with a man who must surely realise by now how totally unsuitable she was for him.

On the only occasion he had brought her into his world, she had spent virtually the whole time hiding, trying to escape the painful sniping of the people who surrounded him. And now a few words in a trashy magazine had the power to wound her to the quick. Without anyone to advise her, Sophie tried to bring herself together, to be strong, to ignore the cruel comments; but the tears kept coming, thick and fast. The painful jibes she had endured during her teenage years were never far from the surface. Now she remembered the beautiful, cool face of the Russian model and, when she thought of the anxieties of her own life in comparison, sobbed at the impossibility of ever competing.

It was a rare night of self-pity for Sophie. Utterly worn down by her recent cares, for all the rest of the long evening she lay there without bothering to undress. She heard Marco knock once, softly, to ask her if she wanted anything to eat. She didn't answer.

By the time night fell, her exhaustion and the long weeks of worry — about her grandmother, about her dad, about Jack, about their lack of money, and now above all about her burgeoning love — had turned into something more sinister. Sophie eventually shook herself out of her misery to undress and crawl into bed, her head throbbing. In spite of the heat of the city, she was shivering to her bones. When she finally awoke from a fitful sleep the next morning, her body was on fire with a raging fever.

★   ★   ★

Jean-Luc arrived at the mill at mid-day. His trip to Italy had been hectic, but successful. He had brought back a folder full of ideas for Céline and Louisa to work on and several new contacts. Business was doing well.

In spite of the success of his trip, he had spent his week in Milan in a restless state. Occasionally, he had found himself in a meeting unable to concentrate, staring down at his notebook, his pen doodling pictures in the margins. When recalled to business, he would snap himself out of it. The truth was painfully obvious to him: he was unable to keep Sophie out of his mind.

Jean-Luc was not generally a patient man. Once he had decided on a plan — and he had made up his mind to win Sophie — he found it difficult to rest until he had put the plan into action. It was this drive that ensured his success, both on the race track and in business. But he was intelligent enough to know that impatience was not always the key to winning. He needed time with

Sophie, and time was running out. She would soon be returning to London.

When he left her to go to Milan, she had been pale. Ever since that disastrous day at the race track, she had been withdrawn. He cursed himself again for taking her there, but the damage was done. Once again, she had been frightened away; this time not by him, but by the heartless crowd who stalked him at these events. Now he needed time to undo the damage, but time was not on his side.

His first act on reaching the mill was to go to her office. When he saw the empty desk, the black screen on her silent computer, his heart lurched. He strode over to the phone and called the receptionist, to be informed that Mademoiselle Challoner's boyfriend had called to let them know she was ill and wouldn't be coming in to work that day. For a moment, Jean-Luc's heart stood still until he realised that, of course, the boyfriend could only be her friend Marco. He strode into the designers' office and asked impatiently if either of them had heard from Sophie.

'Non, M. Olivier,' came the reply. They had texted her that morning to ask how she was, but they had not had any response. He turned on his heels with an abrupt thanks, leaving the girls to their conspiratorial smiles and shrugs.

* * *

Half an hour later, he was knocking on the door of Sophie's room in the student hall. When no one answered immediately, he pushed the door open and took in the scene with one swift glance. Marco was sitting on a chair next to Sophie's bed, studying an open file of sketches on his knee. A large fan was blowing warm air round the room and failing to rid the place of its stifling heat. Sophie was lying under a single sheet, her face pressed to the wall. When she heard Jean-Luc come in, she turned round. Her flushed, damp face rose up in surprise.

Marco stood up. 'Can't you wait to be invited in?' he asked, his expression hostile. Jean-Luc ignored him. He strode over to Sophie's bed and crouched down beside her. Then he reached out one cool hand and felt her forehead. Sophie breathed in quickly at his touch.

'You're burning up, *chérie*,' he exclaimed quietly. He glanced up at the hovering Marco and frowned. 'Why haven't you brought her some iced water?'

'Iced water?' Marco answered in disbelief. 'Don't think I haven't tried. The harridans who run our canteen won't even give us the washing-up water until the canteen's open — which isn't until this evening.'

'*Bon*,' Jean-Luc said, standing up. 'Come and show me where these paragons of compassion can be found.'

He bundled Marco in front of him, his expression grim, then turned back for a moment.

'Is there anything else you need, Sophie? Anything they can get you? Some *pain au chocolat*? A croissant?'

In spite of herself, Sophie rasped a laugh. Jean-Luc obviously didn't know the stern matrons in the canteen, who guarded their fridge from students with all the jealousy of gorgons. Still, she expected they would be no match for Jean-Luc, and she was almost tempted to ask him to procure her some English toast and marmalade just for the fun of it. The thought of actually eating anything made her feel slightly nauseous, though, so she shook her head.

'Some iced water would be wonderful,' she croaked.

He looked down at her thoughtfully for a moment, before leaving with Marco.

Ten minutes later he reappeared, bearing a cloth-covered tray. Sophie's eyes widened. He had not only managed to procure some iced water, there was also a glass of fresh orange juice, its sides misted with condensation, and, unbelievably, a bowl containing three scoops of chocolate ice cream. She sat up, unable to speak, her expression of amazement saying it all for her.

'You should have seen it, Sophie.' Marco's eyes were wide with laughter. Jean-Luc's rout of the canteen ladies had now brought him totally back into her friend's favour. 'It was awesome.'

Jean-Luc set the tray wordlessly on Sophie's desk and passed her a glass of the iced water. Her nightdress was clinging to her slim frame, and he couldn't help but notice that she was naked under the thin cotton material. He looked away as she sipped her drink down, a blissful expression on her face.

'How long have you been like this?' he asked abruptly.

'She started last night,' Marco answered for her. 'She can't talk very well. She's got a really bad sore throat.'

Jean-Luc approached the bed and

bent over her. 'Open your mouth,' he commanded.

Sophie started to back away, but he caught hold of her chin in a firm but gentle hold. Reluctantly, she opened her mouth wide. Jean-Luc grimaced at what he saw. He turned back to Marco.

'Why haven't you called the doctor?'

'I would, but she won't let me.'

Jean-Luc turned a disbelieving gaze in Sophie's direction. She shrugged and finally croaked out a few words. 'I thought it would get better.'

Then she lay back down on her pillow, the effort of sitting and saying so many words obviously exhausting her. For a few minutes, Jean-Luc observed her in silence. Her forehead was dangerously hot, and the temperature in the stifling room did not help. It seemed that the college did not run to air conditioning for their students.

'I think you need a doctor, don't you?' he asked.

She nodded. Reluctantly, she had to agree. After another pause in which

Jean-Luc seemed to consider her and her surroundings, he carried on with his usual strength of purpose.

'*Bon.* You will come and stay with me at my house in the country. I will ask my housekeeper to contact the doctor. My housekeeper will look after you.'

Sophie was feeling slightly delirious. In all of Jean-Luc's typically single-minded plan, only one thing stood out. She lifted her head.

'You have a house in the country?' she rasped.

'Of course.' He raised his eyebrows. 'I go there every weekend. Who in their right mind would stay in the city in this heat?'

Sophie thought of the oppressive London heat and dust, and the faintly rotting smells that seemed to emanate from her estate in the summer. Jean-Luc was right. Who in their right minds would stay there? Apart from the poor?

'Do you have any other houses?' she asked faintly.

'Just my apartment in Paris.'

'Of course.' She nodded.

Jean-Luc caught her note of irony, and his eyes twinkled. 'And a chalet in the Alps.'

Sophie began a croaking laugh that turned into an alarming coughing fit. She sipped gratefully at the water, which Jean-Luc pressed into her hands.

He turned to Marco. 'Can you pack a bag for her?'

Marco nodded and jumped up. Sophie finished coughing, swallowing her water down to glare up at them both, but with less than her usual spirit.

'I haven't agreed to go.'

Marco cast a doubtful look at Jean-Luc, who had assumed his usual uncompromising stance, legs slightly wide, arms folded. He answered her patiently, but with a finality that would accept no opposition. 'You certainly can't stay here.'

Sophie looked up at him, eyes wide and troubled. She knew she needed help. Although Marco was an affectionate friend, he didn't have the patience for the sickroom. But staying in Jean-Luc's house, alone, would be an act of folly verging on insanity. What if he were to guess her real feelings? And if she were to spend any time alone with him, this would be bound to happen.

With a start, Sophie remembered the tell-tale photo taken of her at the race track, and her eyes flew involuntarily to Marco's magazine, still lying on the floor against the wall where she had thrown it. Jean-Luc was a step ahead of her. He had eyes like a hawk. He followed her gaze, and with a lazy action, stooped to pick up the magazine. To Sophie's utter dismay, the pages fell open obligingly at the very article she had hoped to conceal.

Jean-Luc stared at the open page, the frown between his black brows growing deeper and deeper. When he finally looked up, there was such a terrible light in his eyes that Sophie shrank back involuntarily against her pillows.

'My mind is made up, Sophie,' he said, his voice tinged with harshness. 'Let Marco pack your bag for you. You're coming with me.' He threw the magazine with a clang into the bin by her desk. 'And I advise you not to buy this trash again.'

He turned and caught Sophie's expression. Something in her misery caused him to falter. He stepped forward, reaching out one hand towards her, then drew it back, standing just a foot or two from her bed. For a second or two he looked down at her, his expression bleak.

'Come, *chérie*, it will not be so bad to come with me, surely?' he asked quietly. 'My housekeeper will take care of you. I will be spending most of my time at the mill, and in any case, it's a large house. There is no need for us to meet.'

Sophie dropped her gaze to her hands, clenched together on top of her covers. She had been planning to avoid him as much as possible during the remainder of her stay. Now, contrarily, the thought that he might not even want to see her anyway made her feel unutterably defeated. Without trusting herself to speak, she merely nodded.

'*Bon*,' he said. Then, to her intense surprise, and before she even had time to do more than croak once weakly, he scooped her up in one swift, careful movement from the bed, tucking the sheet neatly around her in his arms. She clung on to his shirt, kicking her legs feebly.

'What are you doing?' she wheezed throatily.

'It will be quicker if we leave like this,' he said. He looked at Marco over her head. 'Please pack her bag. We will wait in the car for you.'

Sophie opened her mouth to protest, but Jean-Luc had already nudged the doorhandle with his elbow and was carrying her through.

'Ssh,' he said, as though soothing a child. 'If he forgets anything, I'll come back for it.'

Sophie had no time to protest. Screaming was out of the question, since she could hardly speak in any case. She was left with little option but to throw her bare arm around Jean-Luc's neck and cling on tightly.

*   *   *

Her body felt hot in his arms through the thin sheet. Her pulse was so rapid, Jean-Luc could almost feel the blood leaping through her veins. Too rapid, surely? He looked down into her flushed face. Her violet eyes were on his, their expression anxious.

'What is it?' he asked

'What if someone sees us outside?' Her arm tightened a little round his neck. 'What if someone takes a photo?'

He swept his gaze over her bare arms, the slender neck, the dark hair fluffed around her enormous eyes, and smiled. 'If anyone photographs you like this, you will set a new trend for wearing sheets. Everyone will be wanting one.'

He took in Sophie's attempt to return his smile, to exhibit the same insouciance, but it was a wan, rather pitiful effort.

'You really don't care what people say, do you?' she asked.

They were at the bottom of the first flight of stairs. Jean-Luc came to a halt. He knew she was referring to the magazine article he had found in her room. His arms tightened around her, and he looked down into her uplifted face. She looked pitifully young. Once again, he felt a stab of guilt for exposing her to the comments he found so easy to brush aside.

'No, I don't care,' he said gently. 'The people I care about know exactly who I am. Let the rest of them publish and be damned.'

He began the final descent, his gait easy, still not out of breath. Sophie marvelled again at his strength, both physical and mental, and wished she shared it.

'It's not easy not to care,' she said,

her voice now little more than a throaty whisper. They had reached the glass doors of the building. Her grip was hot on Jean-Luc's neck, and she was looking out through the glass doors with an anxiety verging on fear.

The unaccustomed feeling of guilt which had dogged Jean-Luc ever since their day at the race track deepened. He looked down at her uncomfortably. Every other woman he had dated had revelled in publicity, not caring what was written or said about her as long as her photo appeared in a magazine. Sophie was different. And the worst thing was, if it weren't for him, she wouldn't have been exposed to any publicity at all. If it weren't for him, she would be in a nice, safe student placement somewhere, where she needn't worry about strangers taking photos of her with mobile phones.

'My car is parked right outside,' he reassured her. 'You'll be inside it in two minutes.'

She nodded, meeting his gaze as

bravely as she could. It was while they were both looking at each other — Sophie anxious, Jean-Luc reassuring — that, all of a sudden, the ridiculousness of the situation hit them both at the same time. Jean-Luc's lips twitched. His handsome smile lit up his face, and he couldn't resist a deep rumble of laughter escaping him.

'I bet you've never ducked photographers wearing a sheet before.'

Sophie began a choking giggle, shaking in his arms. 'Stop making me laugh,' she protested, wheezing. 'It hurts my throat.'

'Come on, the coast is clear. Let's make a dash for it.'

He wedged open the glass door and swung her through. Within minutes, she was lying tucked up on cushions on the back seat of his saloon, and Jean-Luc was in the driving seat, making a phone call to his housekeeper.

It wasn't only her illness making Sophie breathless. Within half an hour of his arrival, Jean-Luc had procured her food and drink, organized Marco to pack her bag, whisked her out, and was now arranging for a doctor. She knew Jean-Luc well enough by now not to have been surprised but still found herself stunned by his boundless drive and determination.

Her dizziness was interrupted by Marco's tap on her window. She wound it down.

'Marco,' she croaked anxiously. 'Did you get everything? My mobile phone?' Her phone was her lifeline to her dad and Jack.

'Don't worry.' He dropped her phone through the window. 'And your bag's here.'

He lifted it up then cast a glance in Jean-Luc's direction, who was still on the phone. Marco ducked his head down to the open passenger window, his voice little more than a whisper. 'I'll give it to macho man,' he said with a grin.

It was obvious the events of the morning had now brought Jean-Luc entirely back into Marco's favour. Sophie lay back on her seat, too exhausted to think any more. Dimly, she heard Jean-Luc and Marco discussing her, and the sound of the boot opening to accommodate her bag. Then the engine started up. Marco tapped on her window once more and mimed phoning. She nodded and waved. Her student accommodation started to slide past, a disorientating view seen from her prone vantage point. She shut her eyes.

She had no idea how long the journey lasted, the motion of the car and her exhaustion combining to make her float in and out of sleep. Occasionally, she opened her eyes to find Lyon's tall buildings had drifted past, to be replaced in her line of sight by bright blue sky and tall poplars. When the engine finally went dead, she had to drag herself awake, her eyes heavy and throbbing. By this time, she felt dreadful. Jean-Luc opened her door. The sun hurt her eyes. She climbed out only to be swung straight into his arms.

'Come on, let's get you inside.'

The air felt deliciously cool on Sophie's feverish skin. She dropped her head on Jean-Luc's shoulder. His house, surrounded by trees, was well placed to counteract the effects of the summer heat. Painted green shutters were at every window. The garden was filled with the scent of lavender, and somewhere a couple of chickens were running about, clucking fussily. After the stifling constriction of her student room, with all the noise and heat, the shade and the sleepy quiet were heaven. Sophie sighed.

'Okay, *chérie*?' Jean-Luc ran his gaze rapidly over her face, his mouth set in an anxious line. Then he threw open the door of the house, where a blessed shade enveloped them.

'Marthe!' he called peremptorily.

An older woman bustled into the hallway. 'Here, monsieur.'

Sophie turned her head stiffly to be

greeted by a small figure, a wide smile and features creased and deeply tanned by exposure to the outdoors.

'The poor girl,' she cried. 'Come with me. Everything is ready.'

Sophie was whisked, still clinging to Jean-Luc's strong neck, up a wide wooden staircase. She just had time to make out a view of vegetable plots and a frothy stream through the window on the broad landing before Jean-Luc was opening her bedroom door and laying her down carefully on fresh, cool sheets. A soft feather pillow and the smell of lavender.

'This is wonderful.' Her voice was nearly dead with hoarseness, but she was determined to speak. 'Thank you. Thank you both.' She looked from Jean-Luc to the beaming housekeeper.

She had spent the years since her mother died being the caretaker. It was an unaccustomed feeling to be on the receiving end of care. A feeling which caused hot tears to rise. She blinked them back.

'*Tiens*, mademoiselle,' the house-keeper tutted sympathetically. 'The doctor will be here soon.' She turned to Jean-Luc. 'So far from home, the poor thing.'

Jean-Luc sat on the edge of the bed and took her hot hand in his. 'Marthe will take care of you,' he said. 'And the doctor.'

She nodded, and then he stood and hesitated for a moment by the bedside, gazing down at her. 'I will leave you to Marthe for a while. I must get back to work.'

Sophie sank back on the pillows. Of course, she was keeping him from the mill. She remembered what he'd said about only using the house at week-ends, and realised with a sinking feeling that it was only Wednesday. Did that mean he wasn't coming back until Friday night? He must have guessed at her thoughts, flitting all too obviously across her anxious face.

'Would you like me to come back this evening?'

For the first time that day, Sophie noted a touch of hesitancy in his voice. She remembered what he'd said about them not needing to meet, and wondered if he were trying to tell her he preferred not to come back.

'I am sure Marthe will be happy to look after you,' he continued.

She dropped her gaze to the patchwork counterpane which covered the bed. She was being a burden; and, in any case, she was not at all sure he even wanted to spend time in her company.

'I will be fine,' she said, her voice a quiet croak. She lifted her eyes to Marthe's and gave her a quick smile.

In doing so, she missed the shadow that crossed Jean-Luc's face and the emptiness in his eyes. By the time she looked back in his direction, his mouth was curved in the semblance of a smile.

'*Bon*,' he said. 'I will leave you in Marthe's capable hands.'

He took one of his long strides to the side of her bed and bent over her. For a moment, her world was filled by his wide shoulders and the distinctive scent of him. He dropped his head and placed a kiss on her cheek, his lips warm. With one hand, he brushed the damp hair from her forehead. The urge to reach up and hold him was overpowering.

'Be brave, *chérie*,' he said. 'I will be back on Friday evening.'

With a gesture to his housekeeper, he left the room. Sophie heard their quiet voices outside her door, then the sound of his footsteps striding lightly down the wooden staircase, and then he was gone. She stared up at the ceiling for a while until the white plaster began to blur through her wretched tears. Then she turned her head and hunched herself up under the sheets. She was starting to feel cold. Marthe came in on quiet footsteps and left her a jug of water and some fruit on the little table. There was a shower and bathroom adjoining, and fresh towels. She felt Sophie's forehead and exclaimed aloud. She would ask the doctor to hurry.

Sophie wished she were well enough to thank Marthe properly, but all she wanted to do was shut out the world and sleep. Shivering under the counterpane, she dropped into a restless slumber, punctuated by anxious dreams.

She was in the sports car with Jean-Luc, and they were driving at speed through the congested streets of London. She was begging him to slow down. She had on her violet silk dress, but the fabric was too thin for London weather. The top was down on the sports car, and she had wrapped her goose-pimpled arms around herself. She was freezing. Outside a tube station, she saw her dad sitting on an orange crate, wrapped up in an overcoat and scarf. He looked ill. Next to him, Jack was playing the violin, a frightening expression of concentration on his face. Suddenly, she knew with certainty in her dream that her father and brother had been made homeless. A terrible fear gripped her. She begged Jean-Luc to stop. He turned to her with that implacable look he wore when once he had made up his mind.

'Come, *chérie*,' he said. 'We are going to Paris. You must leave them behind.'

She tried to protest, to tell him she had to go back, that she'd made a promise, but no sound would come out of her petrified throat. Then she was grappling with her seatbelt, trying to leap out of the moving car.

A restraining hand shook her. 'Mademoiselle. Wake up, mademoiselle.'

Her heavy lids opened with a start. Her heart was pounding and her mouth dry. Marthe's concerned brown eyes looked down into hers.

'The doctor is here to see you, mademoiselle.'

Sophie sat up groggily. The doctor was a brisk, efficient woman with round, penetrating eyes behind her wire spectacles. She finished her examination of Sophie and informed her that she had contracted a virulent virus which must be allowed to run its course. The high temperature was a cause for concern, but she was unwilling to move Sophie from a place where she was being so well cared for. She would leave instructions with M. Olivier's housekeeper: if her temperature did not come down within twenty-four hours, she would have to be admitted to the hospital.

Sophie accepted the doctor's diagnosis with a weary nod of the head and a croaked thanks before laying herself back down on the pillow. The doctor looked up from the bag she was packing, and her mask of efficiency dropped slightly. She addressed Sophie with a motherly concern.

'Sometimes these illnesses take hold when we are at a low ebb, mademoiselle. What you need most is to rest and not to worry.' She reached over and patted Sophie's hand. 'Be brave.'

Sophie smiled weakly. She understood what the doctor was saying. Sometimes the body had a way of telling you it was time for an enforced rest. She knew that, but her mind refused to let go. She fell back into another troubled sleep, but this time, instead of the icy cold, her body burned with the fever that refused to abate.

In one dreadful nightmare, her house in London was on fire. She was trying to get through the flames to rescue her dad and Jack. Again, terror had seized her throat. A group of youths in hooded sweatshirts were throwing bottles into the conflagration, causing the flames to leap. Drenched in sweat, she turned to see Jean-Luc approaching, his glamorous Russian girlfriend holding his hand. Sophie cried out wordlessly. The girl looked down at the broken glass strewn across the pavement and curled her lip. Jean-Luc turned, his proud profile caught in the flickering light, frozen in contempt.

She woke in terror, her covers pushed aside. She reached for the cold water that Marthe had left her and tried to force it down her painful throat. Night had fallen. The shutters had been left open at her window, leaving the ghost of a white moon to illuminate the room with soft light. The black sky was covered in a web of stars.

When she lay back down, she felt a warm, masculine hand cover hers.

'Sophie?' Jean-Luc's query was soft in the darkness.

'Is it Friday?' she whispered.

'No.' Now she could see his half smile, the silvery light drifting over his tired features. 'It's Wednesday, the middle of the night.'

'Why are you back?'

'Marthe told me you were ill.'

Sophie grasped the fingers of his hand in hers, the vision of his abandonment of her in her dream still strong in her mind. She looked anxiously into his face. His features were steady in the semi-darkness. There was no hint of the disdain which had terrified her. Then she asked what she had not dared to ask anyone since her mother died. 'You won't leave me?'

'No,' he said simply. He reached up one hand to brush the damp tendrils of hair from her forehead. 'I won't leave you.'

Sophie breathed out, a deep, heart-stopping sigh of release. Gradually, her tight hold on Jean-Luc's fingers relaxed. Her breathing grew deeper. At long last, she fell into a deep, untroubled sleep.

9

At mid-day, she awoke. The room was still in delicious semi-shade, the shutters drawn against the heat. She was alone. For a few minutes, she was completely disorientated. The cool and quiet were such a contrast to her student room, she had a momentary sensation of panic. Then a wave of relief washed over her. The nightmares were over, and she was safe. And Jean-Luc had said he wouldn't leave.

She cast her eyes around the room. The chair was pushed under the dressing-table. There was no sign that Jean-Luc had been beside her in the night. That one had been a dream, too. A familiar sense of misery returned. She forced herself to sit up cautiously and swung herself out of bed. Marthe had hung up the dressing gown which Marco had packed for her only yesterday. How long ago that seemed. She took it down from its hook on the back of the door and shuffled onto the landing. The housekeeper appeared as if from nowhere, a smile of relief splitting her wrinkled face.

'Mademoiselle,' she cried. 'How worried we have been.'

From that moment, Sophie was not allowed to do a thing for herself. Marthe insisted on running her a warm bath, filled with scented oils. Afterwards, she helped Sophie down the wooden stairs to the cosy sitting room, where she had piled cushions on the sofa, and there was a patchwork quilt to cover her. A tray containing fresh fruit was placed on the table beside her, and a dish of icy sorbet pressed into her hands. The icy lemon slid with cold, cold smoothness down Sophie's fiery throat.

Weakened by the exertion of getting up, Sophie could only rasp her thanks, but her eyes expressed a thousand gratitudes. She was exhausted. Marthe left her to rest. The glass doors to the balcony stood open, and all sorts of strange, yet comforting sounds drifted in from outdoors. Birdsong, a cock crowing, a dog barking, and somewhere, the rhythmic sound of a gardener's spade entering the soft soil and being lifted and turned. It was a long way from the city. Lulled by the gentle sounds, Sophie's eyes dropped. Despite her anxiety, the deep sleep she needed to repair her body crept over her again.

Eventually her desperate fatigue abated, and by Friday morning, she was able to take note of her surroundings from her vantage point on the sofa. Jean-Luc was due to return that evening. Sophie felt a rush of anxiety mixed with treacherous anticipation at the thought. She cast her gaze around his room. She had long since realised how much she had misjudged him, and it was no surprise to find that this quiet, comfortable house, far from the glamour of Lyon's city life, was obviously the place where Jean-Luc felt most at ease. The furniture in the room was comfortably worn and slightly shabby. All along one wall, from floor to ceiling, were shelves crammed with books, revealing a surprisingly eclectic taste, from thrillers to old classics. But it was the photos on the wall, in their simple frames, which most intrigued Sophie. There were several pictures of the growing Jean-Luc posing with Marthe and the driver, Louis, who was obviously Marthe's husband. The boy's affection for the pair was evident. In several of the photos, Jean-Luc held one of his many boyhood racing trophies, and the look of pride on Louis' face was unmistakable.

A smaller photo, in a more ornate silver frame, caught Sophie's interest. It was placed out of the way on an oak table in one corner of the room. Sophie had been dying to inspect it ever since it first caught her eye, and in the end, curiosity overcame her. Taking her opportunity whilst Marthe was occupied in the kitchen, she threw back the quilt which covered her and took a few unsteady steps across the room. The solid frame was heavy in her hands. Under the glass was a teenage Jean-Luc, already a handsome young man. Beside him was a woman, who Sophie guessed must be his mother, in her late thirties, one beautiful arm flung carelessly around his shoulders. They made a strikingly handsome pair: Jean-Luc with his neat schoolboy haircut and his piercing blue eyes, and his mother with her pretty, flushed face and immaculate blonde bob. But in spite of their good looks, there was something not quite right about the pose. The young Jean-Luc seemed frighteningly serious and constrained. He was standing too rigidly, with none of the spontaneity of his photos with Louis and Marthe. And something about his mother's wide, grey eyes seemed lost. As Sophie studied the picture, she sensed the unhealthiness in the flush on the woman's features.

So absorbed was she in studying their expressions that she failed to notice Marthe had finished in the kitchen and was standing quietly behind her. Marthe gave a small cough, and Sophie whirled round.

'I'm sorry,' she said. 'I didn't mean to pry. Jean-Luc's mother was very beautiful. I couldn't resist taking a closer look.'

Marthe nodded, but her normally placid features were tight with constraint. Avoiding any reference to the photo she merely let Sophie know, with her usual kindness, that she would bring some lunch for her and a cold drink. So Sophie, out of tact, turned her mind resolutely from any questions about Jean-Luc's childhood.

Mid-afternoon found her lying on her cushions in the sitting-room, one of Jean-Luc's books in her hands, watching the leaves on the trees outside twitch from time to time in what passed for a breeze. A door opened somewhere, and she heard a masculine voice in the hallway. Marthe's quiet voice replied, and then Jean-Luc was in the room with her.

Although he entered quietly enough, instantly the atmosphere changed. He had removed his tie, and his white shirt was open at the neck. His sleeves were rolled up to reveal tanned forearms, and there were faint shadows under his eyes, just visible under his tan.

Sophie straightened herself up from her cushions and smiled shyly. 'Hello,' she said.

'Hi.' He approached her sofa and rested his hand on her forehead briefly. 'That feels better.' He smiled.

'Marthe's been taking care of me,' Sophie said. Her voice, although still husky, had lost its throatiness.

Jean-Luc drew up one of the high-backed chairs and sat down beside her, leaning forward, elbows propped on his knees. For a few moments, there was silence. The soft sounds from the sun-bathed garden floated in with the light.

'I still haven't thanked you for bringing me here,' Sophie said awkwardly. 'I was so ill before, and everything happened so quickly.'

Jean-Luc smiled. 'You know I don't like to wait once I've made my mind up.'

She laughed softly, but her reply was serious. 'Well, I'm glad you insisted. I think I was getting delirious.'

Jean-Luc reached forward and took her hand in his. 'You need to rest.'

'Yes,' she conceded simply. 'I've been doing too much. But this is the perfect place for resting.' She lay back on her cushions. 'It's so peaceful. Perhaps tomorrow I could go out in the garden?'

'But of course,' he said. 'My house is at your disposal.'

Sophie smiled. 'Thank you. It would be lovely to see a real garden.'

Her enthusiasm opened up a whole topic of conversation for them, easing the rather stilted meeting. Jean-Luc explained to her about the house, diverting her from her anxiety with stories of his childhood summers, and Sophie listened, fascinated. Without realising it, he revealed a picture of a solitary, rather serious little boy. His mother had spent the summers socialising in Paris, leaving Jean-Luc to spend the long vacation here in their country house. With no other children in the neighbourhood to play with, he had spent the holidays either fishing, or riding one of the horses they used to stable. Louis had been like a father to him in those days, and it was his enthusiasm which brought Jean-Luc to racing. He would take Jean-Luc karting at the local track and was as proud as any father of all the trophies he brought home.

'And then I started winning serious competitions,' Jean-Luc said. 'And the rest, as they say, is history.'

Sophie tilted her head to study Jean-Luc's expression. She felt as though several more pieces of a puzzle were falling into place. Underneath the formidable will, there was a deep streak of tenderness and generosity towards Marthe and Louis.

Their conversation was broken short by the arrival of Marthe, and Sophie allowed herself to be helped to bed by the housekeeper. The worst of her fever had taken its course, leaving her feeling weak and tired.

As she lay in bed that night, exhaustion took hold, and she felt as though everything she had been frightened of was closing in on her again. Images of Jean-Luc drifted through her mind: the way he had sat beside her, leaning forward, his strong arms resting close to her line of vision; the calmness in his deep voice as he told her his childhood stories. Sophie had feared all along the dangerous intimacy that would develop between them once thrown together in his house, and anxiety filled her. She had shaken off the worst of her fever, and exhausted as she was, it was time she made her escape.

She awoke late, still weak, but managed to drag herself into the jeans and T-shirt Marco had packed for her and make her way downstairs on shaky legs. Despite her tiredness, she was determined to show she was well enough to leave. Marthe was quick to greet her. A breakfast of fruit, *pain au chocolat* and juice had been left for her in the dining room. Sophie followed the housekeeper as she chatted brightly. The dining room Marthe led her into was filled with morning sunlight. A long oak table held her breakfast, and a jug filled with flowers was placed in the centre.

'What a lovely old house this is,' Sophie said.

Marthe beamed at the compliment. 'I've worked for the family for many years, mademoiselle, ever since M. Jean-Luc was a boy. But it's a shame the house is quiet. It's a family house, a house for children.' Her bright eyes were fixed directly on Sophie. 'It would be lovely to see a family in the house again.'

Sophie didn't know whether to laugh or cry at the unmistakable note of hope in Marthe's voice. Her creased features were alive with speculation. Perhaps Jean-Luc had never brought any women to the house before. Poor Marthe wasn't to know that the truth was Jean-Luc's previous girlfriends had all been far too sophisticated to want to leave the city. And far too sophisticated to catch something so unglamorous as a sore throat, Sophie thought ruefully.

Not wanting to disappoint Marthe, she tried to keep her response light. 'Yes, it's a lovely house for children,' she said levelly. 'Jean-Luc was telling me how much he enjoyed his summers here with you and your husband.'

'M. Jean-Luc was a lovely boy to care for, in spite of his troubles.' Marthe hesitated a little before carrying on doggedly, 'He was a solitary boy. A serious boy. M. Jean-Luc is not at all how people write about him in the magazines, with all the girlfriends and parties. He's a good man.'

Sophie was totally taken aback. There was an earnest expression on Marthe's face, totally at odds with the bright, inconsequential chatter Sophie had heard from her up until this point. She was looking at Sophie expectantly, as though waiting for her to agree that Jean-Luc would make excellent husband material.

Sophie was racking her brains to try and find another non-committal answer when she was saved from further embarrassment by the sound of footsteps striding through the hall. The next minute, the dining room door swung open, and Jean-Luc's imposing figure was in the room with them. A wide smile of greeting lit his face on seeing Sophie.

'Feeling better?' His bright eyes slid to Marthe for confirmation.

'She's looking well today, monsieur,

n'est-ce pas?' Marthe's expression was eager as she invited Jean-Luc to admire Sophie. She looked from one to the other of them and carried on pointedly, 'And now I must leave you both. I need to speak to Louis.'

Sophie tried to hide her wince. Marthe's obvious effort at being discreet was unnerving to say the least. Her already stretched nerves were not helped by the sight of Jean-Luc. She tried her best not to stare, but it was hard. His powerful figure always attracted attention, but today was something else. At first she couldn't make out what it was that was causing such a difference. It couldn't have been the clothes he was wearing — just an old, faded T-shirt and jeans. He even had grass stains on his knees, and there was a patch of ground-in dirt on one muscular forearm, as though he had just come in from helping Louis in the garden. And then, as he turned to her with a smile, Sophie finally grasped what it was that made him look so compellingly different. He was totally at ease. Away from the pressures of the mill, from the pressures of city life, for the first time, she saw him truly relaxed. The effect was devastating.

He pulled out a chair opposite, his T-shirt stretching tightly across his broad chest as he did so, bringing his tanned forearms to rest on the tabletop in front of her. She felt his astute gaze sweep over her, and she drew back.

'I'm feeling much better,' she said before he could speak. 'You and Marthe have been more than kind. But really, I shouldn't trespass on your hospitality any longer.'

Jean-Luc glanced at her unused breakfast plate. 'So you're feeling better. Have you eaten?'

She slid her guilty eyes away from his.

'I see,' he said. 'And what about your student hall? Will you eat there?'

She swallowed. Her throat felt dry. The thought of leaving Jean-Luc and this cool, shady house for her stifling room in Lyon was almost unbearable. But the alternative was unthinkable. Her relationship with Jean-Luc was growing dangerously close. Who knew what would happen after a weekend with him in this quiet place? One thing was for sure, it would only end in heartbreak.

She lifted her chin and opened her mouth to speak, but Jean-Luc raised his hand.

'No,' he said with finality. 'I don't want to see your brave face. You must stay here — at least for the weekend — and be looked after until you are eating properly.'

'But I can't stay here,' Sophie said, the huskiness in her voice becoming more pronounced with her protest.

'And I can't drive you back to that overheated room and leave you there alone.'

'Then I'll get a taxi.'

Jean-Luc leaned forward. 'You're being stupidly stubborn,' he said, the cheerfulness totally gone from his expression.

'And you're being overbearing. You can't force me to stay here.'

'Oh, can't I?' Her defiance was reflected back to her in the sudden dangerous glint in his blue eyes. 'Is that a challenge?' Her skin prickled as the gleaming eyes swept over her. 'And what if I take all your clothes from you?' He looked up, eyes dark with threat. 'Including the ones you're wearing?'

Sophie laughed, a rasping, nervous sound. 'You wouldn't dare.'

'Try me.'

For a moment, she met his challenge forcefully, her eyes on his. He had that infuriatingly set look about him. Sophie had no doubt at all in her mind that he would carry out his threat if she continued her resistance. She fleetingly considered breaking down in crocodile tears — that ought to wipe the look off his face, she thought crossly — but she knew deep down she couldn't do it, especially when he had shown such kindness. In any case, what reason could she give him? *I'm frightened I might be falling in love with you, so I need to leave?* Lifting her eyes to his, she accepted defeat.

'You win,' she said flatly. 'I must thank you again for your hospitality.'

In an instant, Jean-Luc's handsome features softened. 'Does it pain you so much to stay here?'

'No. No, you and Marthe have been very kind.' She hesitated before giving him a half-truth. 'I just feel a little . . . well, like I'm imposing, I suppose.'

Jean-Luc accepted this at face value. He rose from the table. 'In that case, we must put you at your ease. Come, *chérie*.' He smiled down at her. 'You asked to see the gardens. Would you like to step outside and see them with me? Before the sun gets too hot?'

Sophie lifted her head with a smile. If she was forced to stay here, she would enjoy the countryside whilst she could. 'Yes, I'd like that very much.'

Outside, in the small garden beyond the dining room, Sophie breathed in the heady air of herbs and cut grass with a sigh of pleasure. The area immediately behind the house had been laid out in a formal style. Tiny, clipped box hedges edged gravel squares and in each square grew rosemary, basil, lavender and a host of sun-loving herbs. To one side was a regimented vegetable plot which, Sophie saw, contained lettuces and the feathery tops of carrots and fennel. A straight path led between the herb patches and vegetable plot to a tiny wrought-iron gate, beyond which was a stream.

'Oh, this is beautiful,' Sophie cried, gazing in wonder at the scene beyond.

Outside the little herb garden, all formality ended. A riot of colourful flowers — some wild, some carefully-planted perennials — continued along the stony path's meandering route, ending in a copse of trees on the bank of the stream. The heady scent of wild blooms was pungent in the hot sun.

Jean-Luc took her hand, his fingers warm around hers.

'Come, let's walk along the path until we're out of the sun.'

Their walk was slow, punctuated by Sophie's cries of pleasure when she recognised plants that her mother had grown in their own garden during those happy years in London, before her mother's death.

'How wonderful all this is,' she cried, looking back along the riotous sweep of the path to the iron gate in its low stone wall. 'I had no idea you were such a gardener.'

Jean-Luc stopped for a moment, looking down at her.

'It was not my work,' he said, after a moment. 'But I have maintained it. Made sure it is kept in the spirit of the original design.' He seemed to be considering how to proceed before turning to walk on. Sophie, her hand in his, fell silent. If this garden was not his work, then whose?

Just before the copse of trees was a

weathered wooden bench, the iron legs it rested on freshly painted.

'Let's sit here for a while,' Jean-Luc suggested. 'Out of the heat.'

The warmth of the sun was increasing, and the short walk had tired Sophie more than she liked to admit. It was a relief to sit in the shade. Out of the harsh sunlight, Jean-Luc's features were dark in the shadow of the trees. He was gazing back in the direction they had come, along the path, to the high windows of the stone house. Sophie didn't speak. She remembered Marthe's remark about his troubles as a child and wondered if she dared to touch on them, to ask him if the house brought unhappy memories.

She gazed at his sombre profile, willing him to speak, and as though in tune with her thoughts, he turned to her, his blue eyes clouded in the dappled shade. But his words weren't the ones she was expecting.

'Did you ever wonder why I gave up

racing, Sophie? Why I turned my back on it?'

'There was an accident . . . ' Sophie looked up at him uncertainly. She had no idea how to respond to the unforeseen question and was unwilling to mention the rumours about Jean-Luc's lack of bravery. Rumours she was quite sure were unfounded. The papers had been full of the incident at the time. One of Jean-Luc's colleagues had been involved in a serious collision on a training circuit. It had been Jean-Luc, following the driver on the track, who had pulled him from his burning vehicle. Even now that image of the young Jean-Luc in the newspaper, racing toward the erupting flames, made Sophie sick with fear. She knew what the newspapers had later made of the incident, and she understood only too well the pain their groundless speculation must have caused him.

'Yes, an accident. That accident was just a convenient excuse for me to quit, a smokescreen for the hungry journalists. At first they couldn't praise me enough — I was a hero, had saved a fellow racer's life and risked my own, and all the rest of it. And then, when I retired at the end of the season — and I was only twenty-four — the stories turned.' Sophie noticed he spoke without bitterness or rancour. He was staring ahead now, calmly dispassionate.

'They said after the accident you were too frightened to race,' she said quietly.

'Yes, but you're being kinder than they were. They said I'd lost my bottle. Some of them said that I was a coward.'

For a minute, that was all. Sophie listened to the cool waters of the stream rushing over the stones behind them. She wondered if that was really all and whether she should break the silence. Jean-Luc was not a coward; they both knew that. There was nothing she could say that could change the stories.

Then he spoke again. 'There was no

truth in what they wrote. I hadn't lost my nerve,' he said calmly, as though for him it were a simple fact. 'On the contrary. I had no nerve to lose. I let the newspapers write what the hell they wanted, because at least it kept them away from the truth. And the truth was that, at the time, I had control over everything. Except one thing.'

He turned towards her now and looked directly into her eyes. 'I couldn't control my mother's addiction to alcohol.'

Sophie's eyes widened with the shock of his words. She stared up at him, unable to speak. With that one statement, the final blocks in the puzzle of Jean-Luc leapt into place. Suddenly, she understood everything with a dazzling, painful clarity. She thought of the photo in his sitting room — the serious child in school uniform and his beautiful, troubled mother — and her heart filled to the brim with the pain of it. To have tried so long, throughout all his childhood and adolescence and early adulthood, to prevent his mother from succumbing to alcoholism; and to let the newspapers call him a coward in order to keep his mother's misery from becoming public knowledge. Sophie understood, finally, how his experience had left him so controlled, so protective, so determined to make sure that the events of his life unfolded exactly as he wanted.

He lifted a hand to her cheek briefly, seeing her compassion. 'I gave up racing because my mother told me, after the accident, she drank to cope with her fear for my safety.' He shrugged. 'And maybe that was partly true. Maybe I did drive her to drink more. At the time, I tortured myself. Thinking, maybe if I hadn't taken up such a dangerous career, she would have stopped.'

'No,' Sophie cried. 'She was ill. It was cruel of her to make it your doing.'

Jean-Luc shrugged. 'She didn't want to lose me. I was all she had. But I couldn't stop her drinking, even when I gave up my career. She carried on. No matter what I tried, she was determined on self-destruction.'

For a moment, she heard the pain in his voice. He gave a brief pause before coming back in control. 'And, eventually, she got her wish.'

Jean-Luc's eyes were fixed on the house which had been the shelter for him, for so many brief summers, from the pain of dealing with his mother's illness. There was tension in his strong profile, and his jaw was clenched tightly. Sophie was filled with sadness for the boy he had once been, the boy who'd tried so desperately to protect his mother from collapse.

'I'm sorry,' she said quietly. 'Now I understand.'

Jean-Luc withdrew his gaze from the silent house. She saw the torment in his vivid eyes, and her heart contracted.

'My father left us because he could no longer deal with it. I tried everything when I was growing up,' he said. 'I hid bottles. I poured alcohol down the sink.

I reasoned and pleaded with her. When I was older, I threatened to abandon her. But no matter what I did, it made no difference. I couldn't control it.'

'You did everything you could. More than anyone else would have done. You gave up a career you loved because she asked you to.' Sophie hesitated over how to continue. At last she saw Jean-Luc in a clear light. His desire to command, to stake his control on the events around him, stemmed not from cold arrogance, as she'd thought in Paris, but from the tragic unfolding of his childhood. There was nothing she could say now that could change the past for him, but she could try at least to alleviate the pain of the present.

'It was your mother's illness, Jean-Luc, not yours. In the end, only your mother could control it.' She saw the frown crease Jean-Luc's brow and carried on steadfastly. 'There are some things in our lives which are out of our control no matter how much we try to direct them. And some things we have to leave to other people no matter how much it hurts us to stand back.'

Jean-Luc gave a tired laugh. 'You have a wise head. But it's hard to stand by when you see the people you love in pain.' He stretched one long arm along the back of the bench behind her. 'I like to sit here. My mother designed this garden when she was very young. When she first married. I have tried to keep it as it was.'

After he had spoken, a silence descended. There was nothing more Sophie could say. But theirs was not the silence of sadness, rather the quiet of solidarity. Sophie sensed the weight of Jean-Luc's tanned arm running along the length of the bench behind her, and the warmth of him, the solidity of his body beneath the faded T-shirt, and the vitality of him filled her senses. Around them were all sounds of life: the bees humming in the warm air, the crickets in the dry grass, the persistent song of a bird in the thicket behind them. For several long moments, she and Jean-Luc contemplated the tranquility of his mother's garden, her lasting legacy, the joyous tumble and jostle of wild flowers and the herbs beyond.

Jean-Luc was the first to break the silence. He moved his arm from where it was resting behind Sophie and took her hand. 'You must be tired,' he said gently.

With his words, Sophie felt weariness flood through her, sagging her body. In spite of her protestations that morning, she was still nothing like recovered. The short walk and the intensity of their conversation had wearied her. Jean-Luc stood and helped her quietly to her feet. 'Come, let's go back to the house. You need to rest.'

10

After the shock of Jean-Luc's revelation, Sophie felt the sudden shift in their relationship. Some of the tension between them seemed to have dissipated, drawing them closer than they had been. They returned, companionably, to find Marthe had prepared them a lunch of fresh salad and cheese. Sophie managed to eat some of the meal and was rewarded with Jean-Luc's quiet approbation and Marthe's beaming smile. That afternoon, however, an irresistible exhaustion overtook her. She was forced to return to her cushions, to lie in the sitting room, letting the gentle view of the garden and the soft sounds from outdoors wash over her. Jean-Luc left her to her rest, saying she must sleep.

But at first, sleep was impossible. Sophie watched the sun lower gradually in the sky over Jean-Luc's garden and thought of that same sun over the roofs of her estate, watched by her dad and Jack. She thought of Jean-Luc's grief for his mother and wished with all her heart that things could be different. She wished her own mother were still with her, and her father were working. She wished she could meet Jean-Luc as an equal, without her burden of debt and the promise she'd made her mother. She wished his world could never touch them, with its photographers and journalists and the harshness she found so intolerably painful, and which he seemed to brush off with such ease.

And then she remembered the magnificent way Jean-Luc had allowed the journalists to tell lies about him, to call him a coward, in order to keep the truth about his mother's alcoholism out of the newspapers. She realised how childish her own insecurities were in comparison and felt some of Jean-Luc's strength seep into her. Sophie felt, for the first time, that maybe his strength could help her stand up to other people. Maybe she could learn to let their petty jealousies wash over her as easily as he did.

As the shadows crept through the sitting room, Sophie began to feel the first stirrings of hope within her. Jean-Luc had entrusted her with a secret about his family that he had shared with only a few. Perhaps, she thought with longing, perhaps his feelings for her were greater than she realised. Perhaps she could lean on his broad shoulders and allow him to work out a future for them both. Perhaps that thought was not too farfetched. And then, despite herself, weariness conquered her, and she fell again into a heavy slumber. When she finally awoke, the sun had sunk behind the tops of the trees. She stretched, still disorientated by her surroundings, and sat up with a start.

'So, you're awake, Sleeping Beauty.' Jean-Luc's deep, quiet voice came from the armchair beside her. His smile flashed white in the gathering dusk, giving him all the appearance of the wolf in another fairy story. Sophie, still drugged by her deep slumber, had woken with a vague feeling of unease.

'Are you Prince Charming, then?' she asked shakily.

Jean-Luc's smile grew. 'I missed the chance to kiss you awake. And you looked so like the fairytale princess. Ebony hair, pale cheeks. And those red lips.'

She had caught her lower lip in her teeth, and he dropped his eyes to linger on her mouth. He leaned forward, and their eyes locked.

'What time is it?' Sophie asked huskily.

'It's getting late. We should see what Marthe has left us to eat.'

'Has she gone?'

'Yes.'

'Where?'

'She and Louis have a cottage. You can see it from your window.'

'Oh.' Sophie digested this in silence.

She had been too ill to wonder about the sleeping arrangements. Marthe must have remained in the house whilst Sophie was ill, but now, since Jean-Luc was home, perhaps she thought there was no longer a need. Or perhaps Marthe was being discreet.

'So we are alone?' Sophie asked, her eyes enormous in her pale face.

'Yes,' he said. There was a pause before he added softly, 'But I am on my best behaviour.'

Sophie was perfectly still. The sunlight filtering through the trees dappled her kneeling body in flecks of gold. In the quiet of the room, the only sound was that of her breath escaping her in soft, regular sighs.

She parted her lips to speak. 'And what if I am not?' she asked quietly. Her eyes did not leave Jean-Luc's as the unexpected question hung trembling in the air between them. For several long seconds, neither of them moved nor spoke. Even the sounds from the garden had ceased. The house was utterly still.

At her words, Jean-Luc's fingers tightened imperceptibly on the arm of his chair. 'Then I will have to behave for both of us,' he said eventually.

'Why?' She dropped her eyes from his to the hands folded in her lap. 'Is it that you don't want to make love to me?'

He drew in his breath, a sharp sound that brought her eyes flying back to his. 'Sweet Sophie, I've thought of nothing else.'

With a groan, he closed his eyes and pressed his fingers to them. 'Don't you know how often I've thought of it? How I've thought of that night . . . ' His voice tailed away in a whisper of huskiness.

'Then why not?' Sophie repeated softly.

Jean-Luc tore his hands from his face. 'And what then?' he asked. 'Can you promise you won't run away from me again?'

Her lips parted, but no answer came.

She thought of her father and Jack, the promise she had made her mother, the life waiting for her in London, and the different life waiting for Jean-Luc. She tried to envisage a future they could share, but could see nothing. Nothing except the here and now.

Jean-Luc watched as her head drooped.

'Is that what you want?' she asked eventually. 'Promises for the future? Can't we just have the present?'

'You have been ill. You are alone here. You are feeling low. Every instinct tells me I would be taking an unforgivable advantage. Tomorrow you would regret it.'

Sophie gave a small, empty laugh. 'So you're being a gentleman?'

'Yes,' he confessed. 'It seems, unfortunately, you bring out the best in me.' A rueful smile curled his mouth.

Sophie watched the regret reach his eyes and let out a sigh, her longing curled up and aching inside her. For a moment, neither of them spoke. Sophie bent her head to look at her hands, neatly folded in her lap. The seconds ticked on from the grandfather clock in the silence.

Then she raised her head. 'Shall we see what Marthe has left for us?' she asked.

He smiled softly, his fingers uncurling from the sides of his chair. 'Why not? At least one hunger should be satisfied.'

Sophie had learnt to find her way about the house during her short stay. The kitchen Marthe had made so cheerful was one of her favourite rooms. A veritable feast had been left for them in the copious fridge. She asked Jean-Luc if they could eat at the scrubbed pine table in the kitchen and he laughed.

'No napkins, no candles, no best china?' he asked. 'What would your grandmother's friends think?'

Sophie felt warm colour rise in her cheeks and turned away. She had no best china at home in London, no dining room, and no choice in where she would eat, apart from their tiny kitchen table. She gave an imperceptible shake of the head, cross with herself for allowing his words to upset her.

'Hey,' he said, caressing her cheek. 'I love to eat in here. And to hell with your grandmother's friends.' He let the subject drop. 'Now, you set the table, and I'll see what the marvellous Marthe has left us.'

★　★　★

In the end, they did have candles — Sophie found some worn-down stubs in one of the oak drawers — and there was fresh salad and fish, olives and bread, soft cheeses and crisp apples. Jean-Luc opened a bottle of white wine and allowed Sophie a small glass. Her long sleep and the sight of Marthe's wonderfully simple meal had caused her appetite to return.

At first their chat was companionable, flowing easily in the candlelight.

Sophie enthused over the salad, fresh cut from the garden that morning. She sliced open a tomato, fat and red from the vine, and offered it for Jean-Luc's inspection.

'Isn't this gorgeous?'

'I wish I could claim credit,' he said, 'but Louis is the real gardener. Every year he produces a miracle from the bare earth.'

Sophie's admiration for Louis' skills led them to talk of the gardener's incongruous love for car engines and racing.

'You already know it was Louis who introduced me to the race track,' Jean-Luc said, his eyes alight with amusement. 'But do you know the strange thing? He is a really cautious driver himself. If he ever lets me drive on the autoroute, he spends the whole journey gripping the sides of the passenger seat and begging me to slow down.'

Jean-Luc did an impression of a man gripped with fear, eyes starting forward, and Sophie burst out laughing.

'Well, I'm not one to talk,' she said, still grinning. 'I can't even drive at all.'

'Can't drive?' Jean-Luc couldn't have looked more astounded if she'd told him she once lived on the moon. 'Why on earth not?'

Sophie shrugged. 'Driving lessons are too expensive. And I couldn't afford to keep a car. But in any case, it's no problem. Everyone travels by tube or bus in London.'

'But you must learn to drive,' he said. 'I'll give you lessons.'

Sophie's smile vanished. She lifted her eyes to his tentatively, to see if the realisation had hit him.

'But of course,' he said after a moment. 'You are leaving soon.'

Sophie bent her head to push at a piece of fresh lettuce with her fork. The delicious food she had been eating no longer seemed as appetising.

'You know you can stay.'

She thought she detected a tremor in his voice. She lifted her head swiftly to find his eyes steadily on hers. The light had been falling gradually, dusk seeping slowly through the kitchen window. The flickering candles gave Jean-Luc's face a sepia glow that lit Sophie from within with a sudden rush of warmth. Filled with wild longing, she leaned forward. Jean-Luc reached across the table to take her face in both his hands, trapping it there.

'Stay with me.'

His voice was low and desperately urgent. She closed her eyes, her slim body trembling with the need that coursed through his body and into hers. She shook her head to one side, a slight, swift motion that failed to loosen the hands that held her.

'Stay with me,' he repeated.

The sound of his voice in her darkness brought back the terrible memory of her feverish dream. She pictured her dad and Jack disappearing in the London streets as she drove by with Jean-Luc, and her eyes flew open.

'I can't,' she cried. 'I can't leave them.'

'Sophie,' he said. He was about to go on, to persuade her, but his voice faltered with her name. He saw the resolution in her eyes and knew how wrong it was, how selfish he was being to keep her. His hands dropped to the table as though made of wood.

'I made a promise,' she whispered. 'I have to go back. When my dad is better. When everything is better . . . ' Her voice trailed away. A sudden draught came through the open window, causing one of the candles to gutter and die. Sophie's whole bearing was full of misery. She rose to her feet, picking up her half-full plate with trembling hands. With mechanical movements, she began clearing away their dinner things, the last of the candles flickering and guttering its waxy fumes above the table.

Jean-Luc watched her, rooted to his chair, his face in shadow. Sophie made her silent progress, from sink to table, and every time she returned, he was sitting rigid in the same position, hands clenched on the tabletop.

'I can't do this,' she said, her voice low with anguish. She had returned to the table and was standing, looking down at his darkened face. 'I can't pretend we're having a good evening, and everything's normal, and it's all going to go on as before. In three weeks' time, I'll be leaving. I didn't want to come here to Lyon because I knew it would all end in unhappiness. And it has.' Her voice broke. 'I don't know what it is you want.'

'Not this.' His eyes had a desperate glitter to them. 'I don't want to sleep with you tonight only for you to leave.'

'Well, what then?' she cried. 'I need to go home when I've finished here. My dad can't look after himself. There are still debts which need to be paid, and they'll only get paid if I go home and get a job.'

'I could pay them.'

'No.'

'Why not? I have plenty of money. Your debts would be nothing to me.'

'But they're everything to us.' Her words rang out loudly in the silent kitchen, and she shrank back. 'You don't understand. Me and Jack and Dad, we've been a unit ever since my mum died. Even if I allowed you to pay our debts, Dad and Jack would never agree. You're a stranger to them.'

Jean-Luc sat motionless. In the jumping light of the dying candle, his lips and the creases at his nostrils were strangely white. When he opened his mouth to speak, the words came with a flat, rasping sound.

'They'd accept my money if you married me.'

As soon as he'd spoken, he knew he'd made a mistake. The words were all wrong. He heard her knife-like intake of breath. Her face was frozen white.

'What do you mean?' The words fell from her lips like cubes of ice.

He rose to his feet, but his usual grace had left him, along with his ability to articulate. It was a lumbering, heavy movement.

'Are you buying me, is that it?' Sophie's knuckles were white on the chair back. 'Are you buying me like you bought all those other girls? A satisfactory arrangement? Is that what you think marriage is about?'

Jean-Luc felt a rush of blood thrumming through his head. He pressed one fist on the table to steady himself. In this maelstrom of emotion, something more was required of him; but, through the roiling mist, he couldn't discern what that was. He felt as he always did when a situation was slipping out of his control. He was a brave man. He had thundered past his opposition on a dark, wet race track, as close to their wheels as a whisper, and stayed cool. Now, at this moment, he was terrified.

He forced his answer through the fear. 'No, that's not it. Remember that day at the race track? I decided to marry you then. That night.' He watched her frigid features, knowing this was all wrong, but stumbled on. 'You said you couldn't face the crowd. If you married me, you'd never have to be afraid of people's comments. You'd have my protection. And you'd be free of debt.'

'You've thought all this through, haven't you?'

Seeing an opening, Jean-Luc rushed in recklessly. 'I know how much your family means to you. Your dad could live with us. The country air would be good for his illness. He could even start up his own business again.'

'And what about me?' she asked shakily. 'My old boss has offered me my job back in London. Have you thought of a role for me, too?'

'Yes,' he said, missing the hurt in her tone. 'You could come and work for me. You've done a great job.'

Sophie closed her eyes. He stood, resting his weight on the table, unable to carry on until she spoke. The rigidity was leaving her body, her muscles easing slowly with the forced rhythm of her breathing. When her eyelids lifted, she was in control. Only the brightness of her pupils hinted at the tears she was fighting.

'Jean-Luc, do you know why I left you that morning?' she asked quietly. 'In the hotel?' She was looking at him with something that seemed, unbelievably, like pity.

He shook his head.

'Everything about you was in control. You were in command of yourself. You had command over me. I was too young, then, to know what it was. I thought it was your money and fame that made you so in control.' She licked her dry lips and reached for her wine glass to wet them. His eyes never left her.

'That morning you didn't ask if I would stay. You just took it for granted I would. You didn't ask if I would come and work for you in Lyon. You just organised it. And now you've decided we are getting married, and you've thought everything through.' Her restraint was deserting her. A small tear trickled down her cheek. 'I don't understand why you never considered asking me what I thought.'

Jean-Luc felt the walls of the darkened kitchen move in on him and recede. He saw her draw back, felt all the fear of losing her grip his heart.

'I want to protect you. Is that wrong?'

'No, it's not wrong. Of course it's not wrong,' she said gently. 'But you can't make other people's decisions for them. You can't insist on protecting me without asking me how I feel.'

'And if I asked you how you felt?' Jean-Luc felt all the fear of allowing her to take control of her own destiny, to refuse him if she wanted to, but forced the question through white lips. 'If I asked you if you wanted to marry me, what would you say?'

'I'd say, I need a better reason to marry you than you settling my debts,' she said, her voice a tremor of tenderness. She let go her grip of the chair and raised her swimming eyes to his. 'I'd say, perhaps if you knew a better reason, you could ask me again.'

Jean-Luc stared down into her lovely face. His dull head ached, and his mind was empty. Try as he might to understand what was wanted of him, the heaviness of their emotional encounter entangled him, dragging him down, so that all he could see or feel was one thing: he wanted to protect Sophie, to keep her safe, to control her world for her. It seemed he had only made her miserable.

For several long minutes, she stood there, waiting for his reply. Bit by bit, his continuing silence drove the hope from her expression until there was only the merest spark of it alive, guttering like the candle between them.

'Then I'll make a bargain with you,' she said softly. 'I will promise not to run away, if you promise to ask me again when you have a better reason. And if you promise to listen to how I feel.'

She held out her hand, above the

dying candle between them, and he took it in his. As he did so, the draught caught the candle flame and gave it new life, flickering high, its light dancing under their clasped hands. Sophie's fingers tightened on his, and she smiled.

'So we have a promise,' she said, her words a gentle whisper between them.

★ ★ ★

There was a ray of hope in Sophie's heart that night which refused to die. Jean-Luc had asked her to stay. Maybe, just maybe, their problems were not insurmountable. And maybe — it was here that the ray of hope flickered and needed a little tending — maybe he loved her as much as she loved him. Maybe he could learn to listen to his love for her, and to put his own iron will to one side to hear her answer. The sun was rising on her future for the first time since her mother died. Its tentative, rosy rays spread a golden glow.

So the sound of her mobile phone ringing the next morning came with a doubly painful shock. It was five thirty. Her brother's name flashed up on the screen, and instantly Sophie was awake.

'Jack, what's up?'

'Oh God, Sophie, I tried to keep this from you. Your friend said you were sick?'

'My friend?' Sophie racked her groggy brain until she remembered Marco dropping her mobile phone through Jean-Luc's car window before they set off. 'He shouldn't have phoned you,' she cried. 'I'm fine. What's been happening?'

She leapt out of bed, wide awake.

'It's Dad,' he said, the words tumbling out of him urgently. 'He's got worse and worse, and then he was out all night and never came home. I was beside myself. Someone found him wandering the streets. He's in hospital.'

'Oh my God,' she cried, struggling to get into her clothes, one hand clutching her phone. 'I'm coming home.'

'And that's not all,' her brother went on. 'He's been hiding all sorts of letters.' His voice broke. 'He owes money from way back that he never told us about. They're going to repossess the house.'

'What?' Sophie shouted. 'How could he? Why didn't he tell us?'

'He said he didn't want to worry us. Said you were studying. And my lessons . . . ' Jack's voice rose shrilly. 'And the end of it is, he's in hospital again. Sophie, I'm so sorry.'

By this time, Sophie was dressed. She felt like breaking down herself. Her head was fuzzy, and her hands were shaking uncontrollably. Her mind was outside her body, trying to control things. Her first job was to reassure her brother. Next job to book a flight.

Jack was ahead of her. 'I've booked you on a flight. It leaves at eleven.'

Sophie looked at her clock and slammed out of the room.

The house was in darkness. She knew where Jean-Luc slept now, and she raced along her corridor and up three wooden steps to come to a sliding halt outside his door. She stood there panting for several seconds, her chest rising and falling quickly, her fist raised, ready to knock. Then her hand dropped slowly to her side. A shadow crossed her exhausted features. Her heart ached with the need to wake him, to ask him for help. Instead, she lifted her head and slowly straightened her shoulders in the old, tired attitude of lonely bravery.

The fatal decision was made. She turned on her heel and went back to her room to gather her few belongings.

In Marthe's kitchen, Sophie pulled out her mobile phone to call for a taxi. Then she unbolted the kitchen door, looped her bag over her shoulder, and set off down the drive to wait in the lane, where the sound of the taxi's arrival could not disturb the quiet of the house.

The note she left for Jean-Luc was short.

Jean-Luc, I've had to leave. I'm sorry. My dad's ill. Please thank Marthe for everything. I'm sorry.

Love,
Sophie.

11

Sophie emerged from the tube station into her familiar grimy neighbourhood, the noise made all the worse by its contrast with the peace she'd enjoyed in Jean-Luc's house in the countryside. Although her heart was heavy, her eyes lit up when she saw Jack there to meet her when she opened her front door. They hugged.

'Oh, Jack, I'm so sorry to leave you with all this.' Her tired eyes filled with tears.

Her brother busied himself making consoling cups of tea. He had been to the hospital that morning, and was able to put Sophie's mind a little more at rest regarding their dad's condition. She took the steaming mug of tea from his hands and studied his worn features.

'I should never have left you,' she

said quietly. 'After I've visited Dad, I'll get all the paperwork together, go through the bills. There must be something we can do.'

'Oh, that,' Jack said. 'It was Dad I was worried about. He was anxious to see you. Don't worry about the money.'

Sophie lifted a puzzled face to him. 'What do you mean? I thought things were really bad.'

'They are.' Jack grimaced. 'Bad enough to scare Dad. But I hadn't shown him this. Didn't think I needed to.'

Jack stood up and fetched a crumpled leaflet from the kitchen shelf, spreading it on the table in front of Sophie. It showed a photograph of the Albert Hall and details of Jack's music competition. He pointed to the section outlining the prize.

'See what I mean?'

Sophie jumped up in amazement. 'Jack, that's an incredible amount of prize money,' she cried. 'I had no idea.'

Suddenly, everything was falling into place. Sophie knew her brother and knew how hard he would have been practising. She also knew exactly what was going through his mind. If he won this competition, all their money worries would be solved. She lifted her troubled eyes to her brother's.

'You know, you shouldn't feel the burden of this by yourself,' she said. 'You don't have to think you've got to win this.'

It was then that the similarity between brother and sister was most apparent. A pair of fierce, determined violet eyes, the same colour as her own, looked into Sophie's.

'Sophie, you've been carrying the burden of supporting me and Dad for years, and if it wasn't for you, I wouldn't ever have got this far. Now it's my turn. I'm going to win for you and Dad.'

Poor Sophie, who never cried and had cried so much in the past few weeks, felt the tears rise again. She looked at Jack with all the love of a devoted sister.

'I think you'll win, too,' she said, her eyes shining with conviction. 'Nobody is better than you.' She picked up the piece of paper. 'When's the competition?'

'Well, that's another thing. I'm glad you're back. Actually, it's tonight.'

Sophie let fall the leaflet, her jaw dropping so far it almost hit the floor. At almost the same moment, the doorbell chimed in the hallway.

'I'll get it,' Jack told his astonished sister. 'It'll be one of the neighbours, asking after Dad.'

Sophie picked up the leaflet again as he left the room, eyes travelling unseeing over the details. By now she was in such a state of tired confusion, it was with hardly any surprise that she heard the curious sound of Jack's voice speaking to their visitor in French. She noted dully that it was a little strange, before the full implication hit her.

She jumped up again and turned

round, heart pounding ferociously, blood burning her cheeks. In the doorway of their tiny kitchen stood Jean-Luc, his body charged with anger.

'How did you get here?' she gasped. She'd sometimes wondered if Jean-Luc had superpowers. Now, in her exhausted state, if he'd appeared before her in a cape, she wouldn't have been at all surprised.

'I caught a plane, same as you did,' he said prosaically. 'And hell's own job I've had of it.'

His strong forearms were folded across his chest. His features were simultaneously weary and furious. Jack peered over his shoulder, a look of consternation on his face.

'I need to get ready for tonight,' he said. 'If it's all right with you . . . ' His voice trailed away.

Sophie nodded. Jack threw one last, shocked glance at Jean-Luc and beat a discreet retreat. Jean-Luc didn't move.

'You made a promise,' he said harshly. 'And I was stupid enough to think you'd keep your word.'

'What promise?' asked Sophie, confused.

'You know. The one where you don't run away — remember?'

'I'm not running away,' she cried. 'I told you. Didn't you get my note?'

'I got some scribbled nonsense. Couldn't you at least have woken me? Told me what was going on?' He took a step forward, brows black.

Sophie edged away from the table, retreating to the window.

'No, I . . . ' She held up her hands as a protective barrier. 'I said I was sorry.'

'Sorry,' he repeated, voice heavy with sarcasm. Then he looked at her, looked at her properly for the first time, and registered the anxiety bordering on fear in her over-bright eyes. Unfolding his arms, he took another step closer.

'Sophie,' he said quietly, then stopped. She was backed against the kitchen sink, her face white. She looked down, unable to meet his gaze, and a light, uncontrollable shaking passed through her body. Jean-Luc drew in his breath sharply and stepped closer until their bodies were almost touching. She shrank away.

'I had to come home,' she whispered. 'I told you. My dad's ill.'

'And you couldn't tell me first?'

'I made my mum a promise,' she repeated like a mantra. 'I have to look after them.'

Jean-Luc looked at her in silence. Her breathing was quick and shallow in the quiet room.

'I know you made a promise.' The gentleness of his voice didn't hide his relentless purpose. 'I need you to explain. Why couldn't you tell me you were leaving?'

Sophie gave a last, beaten gasp. 'You don't understand.' Her sudden, harsh cry pierced the room, causing him to start forward in shock. 'It's my job to look after them, mine.' She put her hands over her face. 'It's all she asked me to do. If you take that away

317

from me . . . ' She gave another wild, terrible cry. 'If you take that away from me, I haven't got anything left of her. Nothing!'

Sophie's slender body, wracked with unbearable sorrow, fell slowly, sliding down until she was sitting, hunched, on the kitchen floor, her face in her hands, her slim shoulders heaving with uncontrolled tremors.

'Sophie, Sophie.' Jean-Luc dropped down beside her. 'I'm not taking anything away from you.'

He pulled her into his arms, soothing her with urgent whispers and caresses. Still her body shook with convulsive sobs until he sat with her on the floor, his arms wrapped tightly around her shaking body. His fingers threaded delicately through her hair in a rhythmic, soothing motion. He bent his lips and kissed the top of her head. Then she lifted her face to his, and his mouth possessed hers with primitive tenderness. He lifted her onto his lap without breaking their kiss and held her tightly, possessively, with all the strength in his body. Her slender hands curled around his neck, and he gave a deep groan.

Sophie shifted on his lap and buried her face in his neck. Her shuddering had subsided. Still, he held her close. Her breathing was quick and warm against his skin. For a long moment, they sat there on the kitchen floor, unable to speak, whilst Jean-Luc's hands moved gently, soothingly over her body. When she had finally quieted, he lifted her head tenderly from his shoulder and reached one hand to brush her cheek.

'Sophie, your mother would be very proud of you. No one can take that away from you. Without you, they wouldn't have survived.'

She stared into his eyes.

'But do you really want to help your dad and Jack?' he asked.

She nodded.

'Then accept some help from me.'

She opened her mouth to answer, but

he held up his hand.

'No, listen to me. I'm not taking anything away from you. No one but you can be a sister and a daughter. But if you really want to help them, ask yourself how much happier your dad and Jack would be if they knew you had someone to support you.'

Sophie's eyes widened. He watched as she took in the meaning of his words, trying to make sense of them, and he took her silence as an encouraging sign to continue.

'Don't you think it would be some comfort to your father,' he carried on quietly, 'if I went with you to visit him in hospital? Don't you think it would make him happy to know you have someone by your side? That he doesn't have to worry about you because you're not alone?'

Sophie sat up straight. She was staring at him, comprehension dawning gradually but unmistakably over her exhausted features.

Jean-Luc had still not finished. 'And

how about your brother? Do you think he wants you to carry all the responsibility alone?'

Slowly, recognition of the truth of what he was saying spread across her tear-stained features. 'No,' she said quietly. 'You're right. I know he doesn't.'

Jean-Luc shifted her gently from his lap and stood up, reaching a hand to draw her after him.

'I should have woken you,' she said, looking gravely into his eyes. 'You look tired. I'm sorry. You must have followed me like the devil this morning.'

Jean-Luc gave a pained laugh. 'As much as I love your apologies, *chérie*, I hope you won't ever give me so much heartache again.'

She reached up and pulled him towards her with gentle strength. Standing on the tips of her toes, she kissed his cheek softly. He brought his arms around her, pressing her to him so that she swayed in his embrace. For several long minutes, they stood entwined, lost in each other, until Jean-Luc tore himself away.

'Sophie, if we are to visit your father, we must leave now,' he said gruffly. 'Before it's too late.'

Sophie jumped and looked at her watch. 'Actually, it really is late,' she cried. 'And we have to get to the Albert Hall as well.'

'What?' Jean-Luc looked stunned.

'It's Jack's competition tonight.' Sophie said. 'That's if . . . ' She broke off uncertainly. 'I mean, if you want to come with me?'

He nodded, gravely accepting her invitation to support her. 'Of course,' he said. Then a smile lifted his lips. 'The next time you lead me on a dance across France, I must remember to pack my entire wardrobe. Do you think Jack will mind if I don't wear a suit?'

'Jack? No, of course not. Jack couldn't care less.'

'A man after my own heart,' he said. 'And you?'

Sophie reached up her free hand and

caressed Jean-Luc's day-old stubble tenderly. 'I think you look good.'

'Well, if Jack doesn't care, and you don't care, who cares what anyone else thinks?'

'Yeah,' Sophie said, a slow smile spreading. 'Who cares?'

★ ★ ★

The afternoon was fast running into early evening, so to cap a day which had already been surreal, Sophie appeared at the hospital in a red, strapless evening dress, ready to go on to the Albert Hall with Jean-Luc at her side, looking magnificent in his rumpled shirt and jeans.

They made an arresting couple as they entered the ward. Her father was sitting up in bed when they arrived, looking frail and weary, but Jean-Luc was right. His reassuring presence imparted a strength which would have been beyond Sophie. Her father was so happy to see her with him, he was moved to take Jean-Luc's hand. They spent an hour quietly talking, and when it was time to go, Sophie noted her father was looking more relaxed than she had seen him in many months.

So when Sophie finally took her seat in the Albert Hall with Jean-Luc by her side, her worries about her family had substantially subsided. She squeezed Jean-Luc's hand gratefully and felt his strong fingers return her grasp. She stole a sideways glance to where he was sitting, relaxed, his eyes flicking lazily over the rapidly-filling seats. Then she remembered their unfinished conversation of the previous evening, and her heart twisted. Despite the trauma of the day, he looked entirely composed. When he'd held her in his arms that afternoon, she'd thought she'd felt his composure break, just briefly. Now, seeing him so controlled, she was no longer so sure. Perhaps his emotional response had been an illusion brought on by her own exhaustion.

She thought then of Jean-Luc's own

admission that day at the race track, that he had been a cold young man, and felt a frisson of fear run through her. She wondered what it would be like, living with someone with such icy control; and whether she should take a leap into the unknown, accepting him for who he was, for good or ill. Then the alternative hit her — that otherwise she would lose him — and both options filled her with terror.

When her brother appeared centre stage, and the first dramatic bars of Sibelius' violin concerto swelled through the auditorium, Sophie gripped Jean-Luc's hand as though she were indeed losing him, and they were both falling through space.

★   ★   ★

Jack was triumphant. Sophie stood and clapped until her hands were numb and aching. Later, as she hugged him backstage, she whispered, 'I'm so proud.'

Jack looked over her head in the direction of Jean-Luc.

'I'm happy for you, too. Really happy, Sophie.' He gripped her shoulders. 'I hope it works out.'

As the crowd thinned outside the Albert Hall, and Jack disappeared to celebrate, Jean-Luc took Sophie's hand.

'Come,' he said. 'Let's walk for a while.'

It was a rare balmy night in London. As they passed through the dwindling crowds, Sophie registered the double-takes and the passing whispers of Jean-Luc's name. The attention no longer bothered her, not as long as she felt his hand on hers. Jean-Luc himself was oblivious to it all. He was striding along, deep in thought, his expression sombre.

Sophie hurried to keep up in her high heels. 'Is this what you call a quiet stroll?'

Jean-Luc didn't respond to her teasing. 'I'm sorry, *chérie*,' he said, slowing immediately. 'I am lost in my own purpose. What must you think of me?'

326

His last words were a muttered afterthought, addressed more to himself than Sophie. The rest of their walk was carried out in silence and at a more comfortable pace.

Hyde Park was a pleasant oasis of calm when they reached it. The waters of the Serpentine rippled lazily. Eventually they found a bench where, in the quiet of the gathering night, they could see the bats flitting over the water and the sleepy ducks ruffling their feathers.

Jean-Luc leaned forward, elbows on his knees. Sophie turned her head and watched his grave profile, the pulse beating at the base of his neck, and waited quietly for him to begin.

'Sophie, I thought a lot about our conversation last night . . . ' He halted for a moment, gathering his thoughts before carrying on. 'It was good to meet your father this afternoon.'

Sophie froze. Was he about to mention her stupid debts again? Tell her he wanted to marry her to look after her dad? And if he did, what should she do? Refuse him a second time? Or fall on her knees and accept — anything so as not to lose him? She stared at him, unable to move.

'Seeing your father's grief made me realise . . . ' He looked at his clenched hands. 'A lot of things have made me realise, if anything were to happen to you, I don't know what I'd do.'

He turned to her, his tanned features pale in the dark of the evening. Sophie met his steady regard at a loss. Was this calm statement a declaration of love?

'I tried to tell you last night. Tried to say the words. But I find I can take a risk with anything except with you . . . ' He turned his face from her so that all she could see was his profile. His body was perfectly still. Sophie rested her hand gently on his broad shoulders and felt his muscles hard with tension.

'I think I know what you want to tell me,' she said quietly. 'It's okay. You don't have to put it into words.'

'Yes I do,' he said fiercely. 'I can't ask you to marry me unless I can tell you how much I love you. How terrified I am of something happening to you, something beyond my powers.' He put his head in his hands. 'Before you, I had put my life in total order. Everything was under control. When I woke up this morning, and you were gone, I thought I'd lost everything.'

Sophie reached forward so that her arms were around him, her cheek pressed to his shoulder.

'Love doesn't have to be about tragedy and loss, Jean-Luc, but even if it is — even if tragedy happens — there's nothing anyone can do to change it. You have to live with the risk. I know you lost your mother — and my dad lost the wife he adored. But do you think that means he wishes he'd never met her? That he'd give up all those years they had together, to avoid his tragedy? If he had to choose, he would do it all again in a flash.'

Jean-Luc gave a half-laugh into his clenched hands. 'Sometimes I think your friend Marco was right. You're too good for me.' Then he lifted his bent head and turned to her. 'I want to marry you because I love you,' he said. 'And nothing's ordered anymore, and I'm terrified of losing you again. Sophie, tell me this is the reason you were looking for, because if it's not, I don't know what the hell else to do.'

'Yes,' she said, her hands reaching up to his face. 'Yes, it is.'

He bent his head then and kissed her. His arms wrapped around her, pulling her close, holding her to him in a fever of love and longing which she returned, at last, with all the passion of her gentle nature.

Around them, the birds called their last quiet songs of the evening. The waters of the lake lapped the shore gently. And a solitary reveller, walking home through the park, was to tell the story for many years, to an unbelieving audience, of the night he had witnessed the great Jean-Luc Olivier declare himself to the love of his life.

Epilogue

A small, dark-haired toddler sat on a rug in the shade. In front of him was an antique toy racing car, lovingly restored to its full glory by his English grandfather. The toddler was beating rhythmically on the roof of the car with a stick he had found in the grass.

'There, I told you,' his uncle Jack said. 'He's going to be a musician. Listen to him.'

The child's family was sitting round a table, enjoying lunch in the haze of the formal herb garden.

'Rubbish,' their friend Marco said, holding up a crayoned scribble. 'Look at this drawing. The boy's definitely an artist.'

The gardener heard them and snorted. 'What nonsense. Look how he loves that car. He's going to be a racer . . . just like his father before him.'

Jean-Luc smiled and looked across the table at his wife. 'I have strict instructions from Sophie not to make any plans for my son,' he said. 'He is to grow up to make his own way.'

Sophie lifted her wine glass in a toast. 'I have a plan for him,' she said, her violet eyes glowing softly as she gazed at her husband. 'He's going to be happy — like me!'

THE END

HOLIDAY ROMANCE

Patricia Keyson

Dee, a travel rep, flies to the south of Spain to work at the Paradiso hotel. On the journey, a chance encounter with the half-Spanish model Freddie leads to the two spending time together, and she suspects she may be falling for him. Then Dee is introduced to Freddie's uncle, Miguel, who is particularly charming towards her — despite having only recently been in a relationship with fellow rep Karen. But when Karen disappears in suspicious circumstances, Dee must decide which man she can trust . . .